BEARDS AND LOVE LETTERS

SYCAMORE MOUNTAIN

MAN OF THE MONTH CLUB SERIES

HEATHER LAUREN

ACKNOWLEDGMENTS

This work is part of a muti author series that I am so proud to be apart of. My fellow authors this year have been so supportive and I hope you get the chance to check out the other great books in the series.

Cover was done by Comar Creative

Edited by the amazing Illuminate author services (Jo you are my rock!) I wouldn't be the writer I am today without you.

Love Scribblers!

You ladies are the backbone of my daily motivation and I hope you know its only with your support I can keep going on bad days. I love you all and I'm grateful to have you in my life.

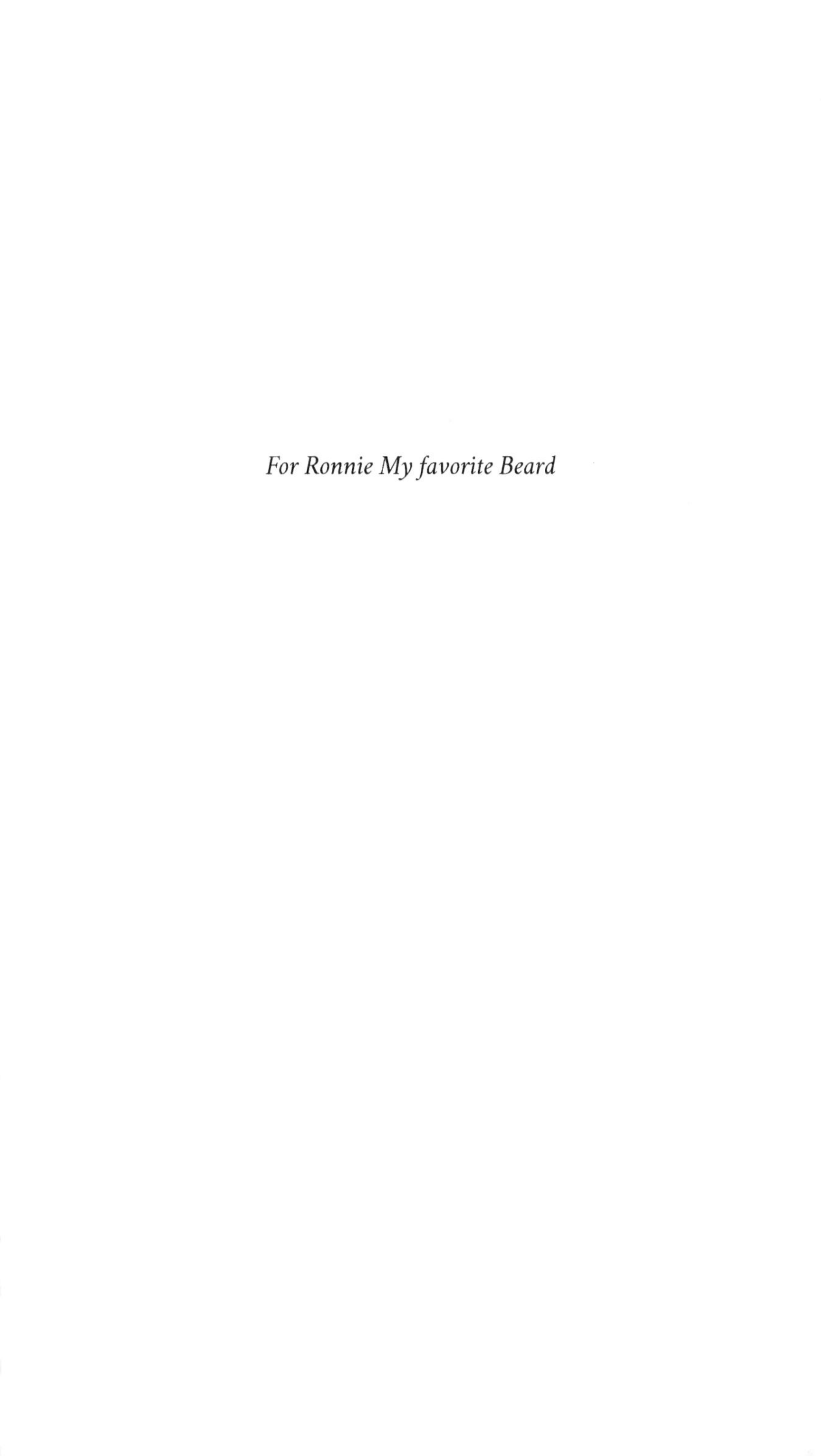

For Ronnie My favorite Beard

CHAPTER ONE

Joey Bennett

"Well, if that ain't the sign I've been asking for every damn day of this trip," I mutter to no one in the empty cab of my Jeep Wrangler as I pull off to the shoulder of the road to inspect what I suspect is a flat tire.

In the last five days of this absurd trip, I've turned around and headed back home to Starlight Bay five and a half times. The half was when I hit a roundabout and circled for a solid thirty minutes, debating if I should take the exit back home or the one that brought me here, to Sycamore Mountain.

Why in the world is a level-headed twenty-five-year-old woman driving across the country, leaving behind everyone and everything she's ever known? Because someone needs me, or at least I feel like he does.

While my mind freaks out with a hundred crazy scenarios of how this surprise visit to my pen pal will play out, I get to work changing my tire.

"Need a hand?"

I jerk, startled by the unexpected question from a woman.

Turning to face her, I wipe my dirty hands on my jeans before stretching them for a handshake.

"Nope, all done. I'm Joey, and literally just moving to town."

"Robin," she smiles, shaking my hand. "Looks like you've had a rough first impression of our merry town. I must right this wrong immediately. Cold beer on the house?" She hikes a thumb over her shoulder at the bar, and I nod, eager for the distraction.

I needed time to figure out what to say to Gavin. Even though it was a hellaciously long road trip here, I still had no idea how to burst into his life after seventeen years of only writing to each other.

"That sounds perfect. Thank you," I sigh, glad for the offer.

I follow her into the cool, dimly lit bar that smells like sawdust but is otherwise charming. The walls are painted black and splattered with graffiti in neon glowing paint, no doubt from drunk patrons.

I sit on a stool at the bar as my newfound friend drops her purse behind the bar. She's wearing a Jack Daniels shirt. She must have cut up herself because it's barely a shirt. This woman exudes girl power in a way I've never been able to master. I like her already, even though I'm equally intimidated.

"So, what brings you to town?" Robin asks, sliding me a glass bottle of Bud Lite.

"Thank you. Um, a friend of mine lives here."

I know people are going to ask this question. This is a small town, so word will get out fast. I figure it's best to play it safe and be honest. Even if I look like a crazy stalker, at least I'll be honest about it.

"Oh, really? Who is she? I bet I know her. I've lived here my whole life."

"Gavin Gold," I say, and her eyes widen.

"What's that look for?"

"Um, no look. Just didn't realize Gavin had friends, that's all."

My heart sinks. Gavin grew up in this town and always told me he felt like an outcast.

"Well, he does," I snap, feeling the need to protect him somehow.

"I didn't mean it like that. Gavin's a great guy, don't get me wrong. I just meant he's not all that friendly. Sexy as hell, yes, but on behalf of all the single women in the small surrounding area, I should warn you he's a little stoic. He's somehow gotten worse since he moved back from California."

I nod. It didn't surprise me she thought this, but she didn't understand Gavin quit nature the way I did.

"Yeah, that's kind of why I'm here. I was worried about him."

"And now you're not?"

"Now I'm more worried about myself," I laugh. "I didn't really think this through as thoroughly as I should have."

"I mean, he won't bite…well, maybe if you asked him to," she winks, and my insides flip. The last thing I need to think about is trying to start a romantic relationship with my pen pal when he's still grieving. I'm here as a friend, only…even if the possibility of more makes the erupting butterflies in my stomach stampede. Hope bubbles in my gut even though I've specifically told myself no a bazillion times….at least.

"It's not like that. We're just friends. Well, hopefully still friends after I bombard him with this unexpected visit."

"Wait. He doesn't know you're here? Where are you staying?"

I shake my head. "No to the first part, and I don't know to the second. My Jeep, I guess, until I can find a place to rent. And eventually, I'm going to need to find work. The life savings of a mechanic are surprisingly small. Plus, I'm still working up the courage to introduce myself," I say, sinking against the counter, readying myself for her judgment.

"Wait, wait, wait. You're telling me you just up and moved here, with no place to stay, let alone a job, and have never met this man? Girl, what were you thinking coming here like this? How have you not met?"

"We're pen pals. We've been writing to each other since a class assignment seventeen years ago. I hadn't heard from him in a couple of weeks, and his last letter was intense, sad, and so final. It took me three days to get everything squared with my family. Then I packed my Jeep. I didn't stop to think about a plan until I hit the highway."

"Wow. That's crazy. I totally dig it, though. I secretly, not so secretly, hope y'all fall in love."

The heart-eyes she's giving me make me laugh.

"There is no way that's happening. As you said, you know how Gavin is."

"I don't know…something tells me you're different."

CHAPTER TWO

Gavin Gold

The bitter coffee smell fills my plane's cabin as I soar through the clouds. The mountain tops are so close I can almost reach out and touch them. This is the perfect escape. Up here, my world is simple. I know this plane inside and out, down to the left propeller, and she practically flies herself these days. Ol' Billy Jean flies like a dream because my Grandad and I built her. The old man would be proud to see her fly again. It's taken me a year, but she's made for the clouds. This is where she belongs. I imagine he's up here somewhere, or someplace close, looking down on us with that crooked gap-toothed smile.

Ivan was a great man and father when I didn't have one and by far a greater man than me. He's sorely missed by his friends and family. Life just isn't the same without him. His great words of wisdom seem to be needed more now that he's gone.

Still, I wake up every day with my chin up, just like I promised.

Billy Jean rattles a bit as I press up the rocky landscape of the Carolina mountains. Adrenaline like this can't be found in any stimulant. My mood lifts, and I pull up the tiller soaring a little too high, pushing this beat-up cargo plane to her limit. It's a game of chicken to see who'll break first. The thrill comes with peace and a sense of freedom. This is exactly what I needed after months of utter depression.

But just when I think I'm breathing above water again, I catch sight of my tattoo.

No more letters, ok? We're not kids anymore.

Maybe stop doing what everyone else wants you to do. Your dad doesn't need you as much as you need him to need you.

I might sound like a dick, I guess. I'm not trying to hurt your feelings, but I've always thought that. If you really wanted to change your life, you would.

You've always been honest with me. I'm just returning the favor.

Have a great life.

Gavin

The last letter I sent my best friend was laced with Jack Daniels, tears from losing my grandfather, and blood dripping off my knuckles after punching a wall. I've never been any good at expressing my emotions, but I could always write to Joey. I'd written her hundreds, if not thousands, of letters in the past, yet I cut her off. I didn't answer her question, **"Who do you think would win in a fight, a yeti or a sasquatch?"** even though it made me smile when I read it.

No, instead of telling her everything, every embarrassing emotion I'm feeling, I cut her off. And I'm sick about it. I hate the feeling it gives me. Vulnerable, weak, pathetic. A fucking pussy is what my grandad would call me. He was a brass knuckle man of the navy. He would not be confiding his feelings in a childhood pen pal.

But Joey isn't just a pen pal after all we've been through together. We shared milestones in each other's lives for the past seventeen years. Even though we never met, I always felt a bond with her. How could eight-year-old me not be intrigued by a girl who, at eight years old, knew her way around an engine? A plane or car made no difference to me. If the girl was still writing me letters when she knew I was a boy, then I counted my lucky stars.

My best friend at the time had just gotten his first girlfriend, and I was jealous as fuck even though I had no clue what being girlfriend and boyfriend meant.

I laugh, remembering I never asked Joey to be my girlfriend even though I wanted to. After third grade was over, we just kept writing. It didn't even occur to us to stop, so we didn't.

After a flight above the town, I land on my runway an hour later and put Billie Jean to bed in the same place she's been parked for the last year.

"Good ride," I say, patting the tiller and turning her off. This is her first flight since Grandad died. It should make me feel better that the old bird still has it in her, but it doesn't. He should have been the pilot, not me.

Jumping out, I secure everything in the garage, lock it up tight, and head over to the house. It's not that I'm too worried about thieves all the way out here, but I'd rather be safe than sorry—another thing my old man used to say. My chest burns with all the memories this place brings back.

Stepping into my office, I sit at the desk and pull a bottle of bourbon from the file cabinet. It's mostly full after my buddy Jasper's last visit.

The desk is cluttered and chaotic, making it difficult to

locate a clean page and a pen. When I finally do, I've also reached the bottom of my first glass. The warm liquor burns on the way down, but it all feels numb soon. I spot the last photo Joey sent me to the left of my glass. It's a picture of her on the hood of a dark Green old Chevy pickup truck holding up two fingers to signify peace. She's fucking adorable. Black grease is on her chin, and her jeans are ripped. But she's goddamn beautiful.

But as I write, all the dark and lonely thoughts I feel cause my words to become aggressive. The drink is strong, and my head isn't straight as I pour my anger onto the page. I spew out mean and hurtful things to her. I lie and tell her writing to her feels stupid when it feels like the only right thing in my life. But right now, I'm angry. I'm alone. It's sad but true. A sick part of me feels good being mad. Suppressed in my gut, now finally free, I lash out, using her secrets against her. Even knowing anything involving her mother would hurt her, I still don't stop. Five pages in, my vision blurs, and I slap my name, Gavin Gold, at the bottom.

My body sways, off-balance as I reach for the envelope, tuck in my letter of self-sabotage, and package it with her name and address. A false sense of closure sweeps over me. She'll never write me another letter. If I know my girl, she won't even reply to my rambling. Nope, Joey Bennett will ghost me. The worst thing I could ever do to myself is push the last person I have in my life away, but that's exactly what I do.

CHAPTER THREE

Joey

The beer starts to taste like water as my vision blurs. My butterflies are a distant memory as I belt out the lyrics of Fancy by the one and only Reba McEntire. I feel like a completely different woman on Robin's little makeshift stage. And if the cowboy at the bar who keeps tipping his hat at me is any sign, I might finally be noticed. Do I want his attention thought?

Hope will float if I don't finish the song with a long, loaded, unexpected beer belch right into the microphone. I don't think twice about it, and as the song ends, I step off stage, tipping up the last of my Budweiser, and head back to my stool.

"This was a great idea," I tell Robin, who could possibly be my idol. She's that fucking cool.

"Coming to Sycamore or getting drunk?"

"Both!" I tell her biting my lip.

"May I have another, kind barkeep? I promise I'm good for it. I'll wash all your dishes or pay you the worth in gold."

She laughs with a kind expression. Robin's not laughing at me; she's the woman showing me what a good time is. I nearly forgot what that was like working for my dad all these years and having zero social life in a small town filled with guys who've seen you in the all-you-can-eat hot dog contest. Turns out shoveling multiple wieners down your throat isn't as hot as some would think. Or maybe, it's just me. Robin would leave with some Jason Momoa lookalike if she entered the same competition. While I might have won, after eating sixty wieners in one minute, I lost appeal with the men in Starlight Bay and tourists alike. The few that were still interested, my brother Reid scared off.

I'm no virgin, but to say I lack experience, would be accurate. Now by the looks of the sexy cowboy at the end of the bar, I could learn a thing or two tonight if I wanted.

My brain thinks it's a great idea.

So why do I keep feeling like it would be a betrayal to Gavin? It's not. We're just friends. I mean, we both would have talked about love interests if we weren't so weird. I laugh to myself at the thought, which makes the cowboy give me a raised eyebrow. Damn, I sure do suck at this courting thing.

I decide not to save a horse and call it a night when Shakira's *Hips Don't Lie* blasts through the speakers filling the bar with a loud scream of joy. Robin pulls me to the dance floor. Believe it or not, I can dance. I think I can, anyway. I'm having a great time, at least, and I move my hips to the beat through my foggy haze.

The trick to pulling off this belly dance is moving your feet. Picking your whole lower half up and into the move at the rhythm of the song. My arms rise with giddy, drunken excitement, lost in a trance with Robin by my side; I almost don't notice the man staring at me until his dark eyes lock with mine.

Gavin.

No mistaking him. I freeze at his expression. He does not look happy to see me. In fact, he is red-faced mad. His beard is longer than in the last photo he sent me, and tonight, he's wearing a gray beanie. Dark eyes tear into me, seeming to see right through me. We finally meet after all this time, and I'm a drunken mess. A hiccup shakes me out of my stupor, and more follow. The crowd is getting rowdy now that I stopped dancing. Cowboy comes up in front of me, blocking our connection.

He's tall and broad and smells really good, but he's not Gavin. My lady engine did not get revved up when I first saw him. Nope, but it's currently pumping hard for the man with steam about to exit his ears.

Why is he so mad? We always said it would be cool to meet. He even promised we would one day. I really thought he would come to my birthday last year, but his Grandpa died, and they were really close. He shouldn't be mad at me.

I stomp my foot and pout at the Cowboy. In my head, I'm frustrated with Gavin. He probably stormed out after seeing me, and I came all this way. The man in front of me thinks it's something else entirely.

"Damn woman, you sure are cute. What's got you so pouty tonight? You want me to make it all better?" He asks.

My eyes go wide at the forward invitation. Where I'm from, men do not talk to me like that. Do I like that? Before I can decide, I watch in horror as he's jerked back by the shoulder and slams right into the fist of a very hulk-like Gavin Gold.

Is it just me, or is there a shimmer in that shiny raven beard?

Even with the music blaring, I hear the moment Cowboy's face breaks against my heroes' knuckles. Wait, is he my hero? How much did I have to drink? What is happening?

In a split second, Cowboy hits the floor, mumbling profanities, and in the next, my burly pen pal grabs me and tosses me over his shoulder. I land with a thud, my stomach threatening war as my head spins from the sudden movement. I take several long minutes and constant swallowing to calm the rising tide of my stomach's contents, but when I open my eyes, I'm greeted with a jean-clad ass of a fucking god. Sculpted perfection, and honestly, I'm too close; the thing must be a masterpiece at the right angle.

Gavin smells like smoked barbeque, pine trees, and burned coffee, and my mouth waters with the urge to taste him. The combination does weird things to me. Stupid things that unfortunately make their way out of my mouth.

As he continues walking, the music fades, and a door closes. The fresh night air is a cool, refreshing welcome to my sweaty temperature.

"Don't be mad. Be glad. This was always meant to be. You're just dumb and didn't come to my birthday party."

"Did you see the video with the one cup, and the two girls? Dude that was not peanut butter. So Gross. Stop me if I told you this one…"

Air rises in my throat, and I push out a burp as casually as possible, then slap my hand over my mouth.

I'll play it off by telling a joke. Distract him. Yeah, that'll be good.

"Why did the sock cross the road?"

Silence greets me as his long strides become a steady rhythm. It's soothingly quiet here in the mountains. I hear an owl hooting somewhere nearby and gravel crunching under his boots. My eyes are so heavy, so I give up staring at his ass. Maybe he'll let me look at it later.

"Hey, can I look at your ass later? I'm so tired, but it's so pretty I don't want to forget it…"

Then the world goes dark, and the last thing I remember is a soft, warm blanket against my cheek.

CHAPTER FOUR

Gavin

God, those fucking hourglass hips were haunting me. The sliver of tan skin when her white t-shirt crawled up her belly. The dip of her jeans, her belly button. Joey Bennett is nothing like I thought she would be.

Don't get me wrong, I've thought about her under me a million times, but I've never seen her before. She was a piece of disposable paper until last night. I thought I wrote her off. She couldn't have gotten my letter. It's still unmailed, next to the bourbon in the office.

My God, Joey fucking Bennett was in my guest room, snoring like a fucking chainsaw all night long, and all I wanted to do was stay up and listen 'cause I couldn't believe my luck.

I don't deserve it, but maybe now, I may have something to keep me out of the bottle. Being friends with Joey sounds much more fun than anything I've been doing lately, and fuck if she's not the sexiest woman alive, just to torture me.

She was sound asleep before I sat her in my truck. I talked to Robin and was fucking furious to know Joey was planning on sleeping in her car last night. She has never backed down from anything, and not coming to me first feels shitty. Piece of paper or not, she's my best friend, and I want her safe under my roof, not in some sketchy bar parking lot.

Although rationally, I know Robin would have taken care of her, I didn't want that. I wanted to be the one to take care of her. Protect her from assholes dressed up like rodeo stars trying to pull tail in dive bars when they roll through town. Motherfucker deserved a lot more than the one punch he got, but I needed to get her out of there. My blood was volcanic. I erupted like a jealous lover, but fuck if I'll apologize. No way on God's green earth will I ever apologize for my actions last night. That sleazeball put his hands on her without asking; that shit doesn't fly in my book.

If she's pissed at me when she gets up, I'm prepared.

With no chance of getting any sleep at all, I cleaned the place spotless last night. Made sure blankets were by the couch and brought out some of the candles I use when we lose power out here. We're not in the city, so it happens a few times a year and can be unpredictable. I have a backup generator, but some smell nice, and I'm hoping she'll like them.

Yeah, dumbass, she'll stay 'cause your house smells nice.

I roll my eyes at myself but place a few more above the fireplace. I've also made a shit ton of pancakes and went out early to grab eggs and blackberries fresh from the garden that grows wild on the west side of my inherited property.

I mentally high-five myself for getting the honey from Ms. Doris and wonder if Joey would like the Farmer's Market.

Just as the coffee pot beeps, a blood-curdling scream comes from her room, sending a cold shiver up my spine and instantly causing my chest to ache. Is she ok? I take off in a sprint and take the stairs two at a time. When I reach her room, I don't bother with the door handle, all I can think about is getting to her as fast as possible, so I plow through it. With my weight behind it, the force of my shoulder sends the door off its hinges and the frame splinters. Inside, I find a shell-shocked Joey, with wild raven hair sticking out around her soft face. She screams again, this time at me, and then I notice Billy the Kid in bed beside her. A chunk of her hair in his mouth.

"Damn it! No! Down! Wrong room, you crazy goat." My growl is weak as my four-legged friend kicks out of the blankets he's shared with Joey, seemingly all night. She's looking at me like I'm nuts leaving with the animal. I wonder what is more jarring in her hungover state. Laughing quietly to myself, I take the intruder back to my new room, the master bedroom, and lay him on the dog bed in the corner. I'll leave the door propped open, but he usually sleeps in.

"Friend of yours?"

Joey stands with her back to me, pouring herself a cup of coffee, and I take a moment to center myself. My eyes travel down her long messy hair to her snug waist and ample backside. Fuck what I wouldn't give to bite that fucking cheek right now. Fall to my knees and sink my teeth…

I clear my throat, feeling like an even bigger asshole. She's my best friend, and I'm gonna keep my hands to myself. I say those words forgetting the reasoning as she turns and those bright hazel eyes lock with mine. Her tongue licking her lip forces me to break the spell. I wonder if they taste like coffee.

"Yeah. Sorry about him. That room used to be mine. My little buddy is spoiled around here, now that it's just me. I'll keep him in my room, though. He shouldn't bother you again."

"He didn't bother me, just scared me. Plus, you hulking out was kind of unexpected as well…oh, and the whole drinking way too much and feeling terrible is not helping."

"Yeah, I imagine, but it does serve you right for not coming here first."

Her face sobers. Gone is the snark, replaced by embarrassment.

"Last night was not at all what I wanted for our real-life meeting." She shakes her head, and the look she gives me makes me want to go slay a Dragon. Anything to make it better.

"I'm not sorry for protecting you, Joey. This wasn't what I wanted either, but what the hell were you doing? After all this time, you suddenly come to visit? Oh, but stop off to get hammered and not make it all the way to my house?"

Damn it. That's just making it worse. Tears fill her eyes, and my chest breaks open and threatens to spill all the secrets I've kept locked away. The ones about her. They're the only ones she doesn't already know.

"Hey! At least I showed up!"

Fuck! She got me. I fold and take a moment to calm down. I wanted to meet her so bad I finally couldn't take it. I made a plan and sold a bunch of my shit. Then got a short-term gig flying tech guys out of Silicon Valley to meetings around the world. Thanks to a client, I got a place in California and was gonna be financially set to take a trip anywhere. First stop, Starlight Bay, to pick up Joey, then together, we were going to soar the skies until the gas ran out. Stopping for new adventures along the way. Unfortunately, I met the woman of my nightmares in the form of a roommate. She was supposed to help pay the insane utilities but caused so much damage to my rental that I left with almost nothing.

Then my mom called to tell me my grandpa had passed, leaving me everything. She told me I needed to come home, and I didn't fight it. I wrote Joey and told her a vague version of what happened, how he had a heart attack, but my letters got shorter, and the last one I sent was weeks ago. Guilt washes over me like a familiar skin.

"You put yourself in danger, and I wish you wouldn't have come!" I shout at her, hating it instantly.

She shakes her head at me. "I don't think that's true, and if it is, I've lost my best friend today."

Ouch. Her words stab me right where it hurts. "But I think I know you by now, and you're just being an asshole because that's your fallback. It's not ok, and if you really don't want me here, I'll leave. I just need a ride back to my car."

"No." I shake my head frantically. "I'm sorry."

I take a step toward her, afraid she'll disappear. Keeping my hands to myself, I switch tactics. I've never been good with words anyway. I grab the breakfast tray I have ready with a wild rose, buckwheat pancakes with banana slices and almonds, scrambled eggs, and bacon beside a fresh cup of orange juice.

"Wow. All this for me?"

I nod in reply, too afraid to speak in case something stupid comes out of my mouth.

"Thank you." Her face softens, and that smile I've longed for finally spreads across her face.

My chest loosens, and I'm finally able to calm down as she sits at the table. I unload the plate and juice in front of her, returning to the coffee pot for a cup. When I make it back to her, a warm sense of pride fills me, watching her enjoy the bite she's chewing. She looks at me with so much adoration over the meal I feel ten feet tall.

"No one has ever cooked for me before," she says, looking down at her plate. My pride turns to anger at every man that didn't make her feel special. A part of me feels glad. I want to be that man. But how can we cross that line? We just met.

"I'm honored to be your first." It is easy to say because it's her. Something about the plate draws my attention, and I focus on the leaf pattern rather than looking at her with the raw vulnerability I feel.

I tell Joey everything, always have, but somehow it's harder standing in front of each other, not being able to hide behind the pieces of paper we usually rely on.

CHAPTER FIVE

Joey

*I*t's weird; no denying it. This long, stretched silence is awkward, but luckily my plan seems to have worked itself out. Not ideally, but now I don't have to worry if he wants me to show up here or not. Despite his outburst and the shy smile he's trying to hide, I think I'm going to be ok.

We hear Billy the Kid cry out from the other room, and my heart constricts.

"Couldn't we let him out?"

"I thought he bothered you?"

"Bothered is a strong word. I was in shock waking up in your bed."

I let that part hang, testing the waters.

"Your bed. If you want it. Mine's down the hall."

Well, that's not exactly an invitation to wild hot sex, but the bed is better than my car. I shake my musings away as I remember my goal. Get the guy to see me as a woman, not just his friend. Then maybe sex would be invited. My stomach turns with nerves at the thought. I can totally pull off this seductress thing. Maybe. I hope.

I watch him walk away from the table, and when he comes back, it's with my intruder in his arms. The sight sends an unexpected warmth to my center so fast that I'm forced to clench my legs together.

"Here, eat," Gavin orders the tiny Billy Goat, who obeys, eating something in a big dog dish. "He's a runt. I shouldn't keep him, but the clever critter won me over. Now he keeps sneaking into the house. Kinda won me over with his smarts."

"Aww."

That deadly smile stretches across his face, and mine matches. Something about making Gavin smile does unexplainable things to my insides. At that moment, I make it my new mission to make him do it again.

"Anyway, eat. I thought you might want to check the place out."

There's no question in his tone but in his swirling dark eyes. Do I do that to him? Is he nervous?

"Ok, Daddy, anything else?"

He s grunts at my smart-ass reply, but we quickly eat our breakfast, which consists of the world's greatest pancakes, and much-needed Tylenol, then head out on his Four Wheeler.

The air smells of pine, and the wind whips against my face as we ride, and I take in the Gold property. A rolling valley sits nestled into the mountains, and in the distance, I can see a glittering airstrip and a large warehouse. Lush green plants, and to my delight, wildflowers cover the land. It's amazing how something so delicate can survive the harsh climate of the mountain, and the thought reminds me of my friendship with the now grown man I'm plastered to the back of. He might sound gruff to most, but inside, my best friend is as delicate as a flower. He's hurting even now. I wish he would share more of himself in real life and not just on paper. At breakfast, it seemed like we were falling back into our comfortable pattern, but I realize it's going to take some time. And if this ride is any indication, I will have a lot of fun in the meantime.

Adrenaline rises as he takes a sharp turn into the tree-lined forest.

"Do you trust me?"

"Yes, Aladdin, I trust you!" I yell, bouncing behind him. We both have a fondness for the movie and once wrote each other quotes from our favorite scenes. He also loved the Princess Bride but really, who doesn't? If someone says they don't, they are lying their faces off and shouldn't be trusted.

"Hold on!" He yells back just as the ground in front of us disappears, and suddenly, we're speeding down a dirt trail. Steep and rocky, tall pine trees on either side. I'm in good hands, Gavin is capable and knows this land 'cause it's his backyard. His own personal playground, and he's taking me out to play. I laugh with excitement as we swerve around boulders and stumps I would never have seen, all at a crazy speed.

As much as I might trust him, I'm also scared every time he takes a sharp turn. I feel his chest rattle with laughter as we take a steep hill, and I cling to him as tight as I can. I wrap my legs around his waist, and I'm not even a little embarrassed about it. I'm terrified but also having the best time of my life.

After a minute, we slow down and reach a field with tall grass and colorful butterflies fluttering around. It's beautiful, like something from a fairy tale. The field ends at a waterfall. A large natural spring from the surrounding mountainside.

Like a painting, the running water glistens, lush green moss, and small wildflowers sprout everywhere. Birds chirp, and the engine purrs as we continue to the water's edge.

My heart syncs with the rhythm of the waves crashing into the rock. A mist hangs by our feet, and I mentally wonder where the men playing the violin are because this is too perfect.

"Wow, this place is amazing!" I yell until he cuts the engine.

"Beautiful, isn't it? Remember that drawing I made you? Told you I'd show you some day."

I choke at his sentiment. Grateful for his back as I wrestle with my stupid feelings.

But what if this could be more? What if he saw me as more than a friend?

"Thank you." That is all I manage to say, but I hug his back, hoping my action is louder than words, not because I'm scared for my life anymore, but because he brought me here. A place I alone know he escapes to when he's feeling too much. My proud friend has a bad habit of holding everything in and not talking about issues that bother him. Instead, he comes here.

CHAPTER SIX

Gavin

Her breasts pressing against me warms my back. Her strong legs squeeze my thighs at every bump in the road. I may have taken the roughest trail to the waterfall for a reason, but I'll never admit it. Just having her here with me feels like the dark cloud I've been walking around with since Grandad died has evaporated, leaving nothing but her sunshine.

Up ahead by the airstrip, a large puddle sits, daring me. Looking down at our clothes, I confirm both our jeans are already splattered with mud from the ride, so I take a chance and hit the gas.

"Hold on!"

All four wheels spraying water up all around us and raining down. Her scream is part excited, part terrified, and all I can do is laugh as we splash through the muddy water. I turn and plow through it again and again. Each time she laughs and hugs my thighs with hers, which I am acutely aware of. It's been years since I've laughed this much, and honestly, even then, it was probably at something she wrote me in a letter. The last thing I want to do is lose the one person who brings me any happiness. I can't mess up our friendship. I might want her more than anything, but all we can be is friends.

When the puddle is mostly bare, thanks to my tracks, I slowly drive back home. My grandfather's two-story cabin sits in pristine condition with all the modern bells and whistles. Around back, I park the beast and kill the engine. We're still out of breath from the adrenaline, but we can't help but laugh.

"That was the most fun I've ever had."

"Whatever, liar. You can't tell me Starlight Bay doesn't have mudding."

"What-ing?"

"Seriously? There are people in a small town somewhere that don't know the joy of killing time on back roads splashing through muddy water and rippin' up earth?"

"Um, yes. Starlight Bay is a beach town. We do boat block parties and bonfires."

"Ok, I can do a bonfire. Might have to run down into town for smores. Anything you need?"

That was casual, right? Nothing in my words screams, 'please never leave,' right?

"Yeah, there are a few things I'd like to grab, my car being one of them."

I nod and head to the side of the house to park.

"You have an outdoor shower!"

Joey's off my four-wheeler and walking towards the greenhouse where there is indeed a shower.

"Sure do. Didn't realize that would impress you, or this would have saved me hours."

Lie. I'd never under any circumstances want to be anywhere than with her. If she's an option, she's always my first choice.

"Dibs!" she says and runs off. To my shock, she reaches down and pulls her t-shirt off. Her back is to me, but I watch with rapt attention. The black sports bra is next, and then her belt. Just as she's wiggling her hips, she moves behind the wall. One of three that gives just a little privacy. I growl my frustration into my fist, questioning our life-long friendship. A friend would not strip in front of the other…

Or am I so far in the friend zone she doesn't care if I see her naked or not?

"Towels are hangin' on the rack on the far wall," I shout over my shoulder, stomping to the back door, irrationally mad. At who is anyone's guess? My dick more than likely. If he wasn't interested, my life would be a million times easier right now. Being her friend wouldn't be physically painful, for fuck's sake.

Cleaning up quickly, I calm myself down and throw on dark jeans and a button-up. Not sure why I choose it over my regular t-shirt, I just do. Got nothing to do with going into town with her at my side. We're just friends. Doesn't matter what folk's opinions will be.

Coming down the stairs, my eyes dart to the window, and at just the right angle, Joey Bennett stands before me, butt naked. Streams of water from the copper faucet flow down her tan body like a small river. She's humming a song I don't recognize, but it's enough to shake me out of my frozen stupor.

After scolding myself for being a pervert, I continue to think about her body. My mind relentlessly stuck on the image. She doesn't have tan lines. Did that mean she sunbathes naked? Fuck, the thought of what her front might look like has me growling when she finally walks into the cabin in only a small white towel.

"Best shower ever."

"Glad you like it." I sure as hell did. "Feel free to make it your own if you want."

"Thanks. Does this mean you'll let me stay?"

Was she serious? My mind is foggy from her being so close and wearing so little.

"You want to stay?"

"Um, well yeah, not really looking to tuck my tail between my legs and drive all the way back home?"

"You're welcome to stay, of course."

"Tell you what. If I cramp your grumpy style, just let me know, and I'll move down the hill, ok?"

"The hill?" I say, ignoring the clench in my gut at the thought.

"Mountain," she says, shrugging her small shoulder. The movement threatens to untie the flimsy towel. "It's a mountain, beach girl, remember? I'll get all the lingo, eventually."

"Ok. You do that." I can't help but snicker at her.

Raven locks fall out as she bends over to dry her hair, and I turn back and grab my keys to distract myself from watching her.

For a woman, Joey is what folks would call low maintenance, but that's always bothered her. In my eyes, being a simple woman doesn't make her any less beautiful. From her silky hair to her dark eyes and full lips, she's always revved me up. Even as a kid with the first photo she ever sent me, I think my exact words were "wow" and "holy shit" 'cause she was prettier than I thought she would be. As a kid, I had never met a girl who liked the things that interested me. That might be why my relationships over the years never went further than a date or two. The fact I already had a major crush on my pen pal meant girls literally had big boots to fill.

Hard not to compare every woman to your best friend when she's as gorgeous as Joey. I've always loved her passion for engines and the joy she gets from restoring something broken to something her fellow man finds value in. Joey is a people pleaser, whether or not she realizes it. She's always done what's expected of her…until now.

CHAPTER SEVEN

Joey

Shopping in Sycamore Mountain is interesting, to say the least. Cute boutique shops with tourists fluttering in and out line each side of the brick street. Gavin is walking like an impenetrable wall beside me. I didn't realize how quiet he was in real life. I guess I just assumed he'd be just as comfortable talking to me as he is writing, but it's not been easy. All I've gotten are lots of one-word answers to the point I feel like I might be annoying him. The silence isn't uncomfortable, so I take solace in that as I dip in and out of small shops. He takes a few steps before realizing I'm not beside him but watching that big flannel-wearing mountain man back step with wide eyes has me giggling.

Inside a dark tattoo shop, I'm greeted by the familiar sounds of Metallica and start singing the lyrics. It gains me a funny look from Gavin, who looks like he'd rather be anywhere else.

"What's wrong? You always said you wanted to get a tattoo."

He just grunts and looks at his boots.

"Hey, sorry folks, we don't have time for a walk-in at this time, but you're welcome to get on the books." A good-looking guy with colorful art up and down each arm says.

"Gavin? That you? What's up, man? Come to match up the butterflies?" He laughs, but what the fuck does that mean?

"What butterflies?" I grin.

"Nothin', let's just go. We'll call you, Nolan," Gavin says, nodding his goodbye as he walks out of the shop.

Well, I sure as hell am not done with this conversation, he clearly doesn't want to have. I take off after him after Nolan and I exchange matching looks of confusion.

"Hey!" I shout down the sidewalk, speed walking to catch up with him.

"Hey, what?"

"What the hell was that back there? Do you have a tattoo or something? It's not a big deal. I mean, I'm butt hurt 'cause that was supposed to be *our* thing, but I think I'll survive it. What I won't stand for anymore is you not talking to me. Grunts don't count, Gavin." I hold up a finger and stop in front of him, halting his escape.

"Yeah."

I raise an eyebrow. He groans, kicking a rock, not looking at me. Standing my ground, I stay silent and stare expectantly.

"Yeah, I do alright, and yes, it was meant to be an *us* thing, and I fucked up."

The way he says it is so defeated, like everything between us is just done in one action, which is stupid.

"So why is that a big enough deal you stomped out of there like a toddler?"

"It's not. Drop it." His tone is clipped and harsh.

I rear back in shock. "What's that now?"

"Fuck. I'm making it worse." He grabs his beanie, pulls it off, running his hands through his dark black hair. His frustration with himself is boyish and so adorable I almost forget I'm mad at him.

We're both quiet for a moment. Just long enough to get spotted in a small town.

"Hey, guys!" Robin says, breaking into our awkward bubble.

Gavin huffs and puts his beanie in his pocket.

"Hi."

"I just interrupted something, didn't I?" She cringes, and I shrug.

"What's up?"

"I just wanted to invite your bearded friend here to come to this year's battle of the beards."

"No." He grunts.

"Ok, bye." She laughs, clearly uncomfortable.

I roll my eyes. "When is it?"

"No." He grumbles, but if Gavin really thinks I moved here just for him, he is sadly mistaken. Wounded heart or not, I don't take orders, and I promised myself to do more things outside my comfort zone. Everything about Robin is out of my comfort zone, even though I love her already.

"I guess it'll just be me then," I say, standing taller, making my point very clear.

"Joey." His tone is warning.

"So, I'm just going to go…" Robin says, slowly backing away. "The battle's at the bar tonight around nine…, Joey. Would love to buy you a beer.

"You're evil," I reply, squinting at my former new friend.

She just cackles, turning and crossing the street.

The ogre beside me grumbles something I miss, and my

attention snaps back, reminding me that he's still keeping something from me.

"We don't have secrets," I snarl at him.

His posture instantly rights with a growl, and that strong glare pins me in place. Embarrassment over being so turned on by his growl paints my cheeks. Intense heat rushes to my core, and I'll be damned, I fucking wet my panties.

Then he grins.

Fuck me. Does he know what he's doing to me?

I clear my throat expectantly. Crossing my arms so he knows I'm not backing down easily.

The former growly bear softens in front of my eyes.

"You're right. I have been keeping a secret, but I'm not sure you want to know this one."

Emotion I never expected laces his voice, and it almost pains me.

"If it's about you, I want to know. You don't have to tell me here in the middle of town, but I didn't move here, so you could give me two-word answers to shit and run out of places without me."

"I'm sorry, Joey. I acted like a jackass."

That very rare smile is back on his handsome scruffy face, and I can't help but smile back. We're good. Whatever the secret is, our friendship will survive. I just have a feeling.

***

"LADIES AND GENTS, it's with the greatest pleasure that I introduce this year's battle of the beards!" Robin yells into a microphone, kicking off a bellow of screams from the rowdy crowd. Men with varying lengths of facial hair step up to the stage.

Pour Decisions is packed with locals and tourists alike.

And here I thought only my corky little town celebrated silly things like World Beard Day.

Gavin grabs my hand, guiding me through the crowd until we get to a booth. The gesture means more to me than he knows and gives me the added courage to take off my jacket. It's nothing huge, like a sexy dress and heels, but I'm wearing a fucking push-up bra, which is new to me. It makes me feel sexy, and my boobs look awesome.

All afternoon I'd thought about it. Gavin and I never talked about boyfriends or girlfriends, but I always suspected he had had dozens of girls through the years. Just the thought made me irrationally jealous, and honestly, my biggest fear is that he only sees me as a friend, not a woman.

But fuck it. I'm brave now; I came all this way. He didn't kick me out, so I put on the damn push-up bra under a black tank top. A simple rose gold chain with a wrench and another longer chain with a blue butterfly hangs around my neck. I've always loved butterflies, but it's probably the only girlie thing about me growing up, so I never told anyone but Gavin.

I take a deep breath as he settles into his seat and waves to the girl behind the bar. He's wearing a sexy navy blue button-down that hugs every rippling muscle. He trimmed his beard, and it shines with oil that smells musky and good enough to eat.

My panties were instantly wet when I opened the guest room door to leave. I felt way underdressed. It's like, for the first time in my life, I wish I had been dressed to the tens like the heroines in romantic comedies who had a glamourous makeover, and when the hero takes one look at her coming down the stairs, boom, he knows he loves her. Granted, that's dramatic, but this is that epic moment for me…here goes nothing.

My jacket falls down my shoulders, and a cool breeze

blows against my skin. Gavin's eyes widen, and his jaw flexes with tension as goosebumps erupt on my skin. I press my luck and put my elbows on the table, pushing my boobs together, on full display for him. Nervously, I chew my lip, hoping he'll say something. He still hasn't told me his secret, but I can tell he's trying. I caught him pacing the porch waving his hands around like he was trying to explain something. It did nothing to help the growing crush I'm harboring, and maybe tonight, I can push just a little, just to see if he might actually be interested without demolishing my heart.

CHAPTER EIGHT

Gavin

I struggle to focus on anything as Joey leans over the table in her low-cut tank top. My eyes laser focus on the blue butterfly between those tempting peaks begging me to help it out. With my mouth. At least in my head, anyway.

My brain is foggy with fantasies, so when my name is announced, I don't protest in time, and suddenly, I'm being dragged up to the stage by Robin and Gage. If it weren't for the ex-military man, I would have easily pulled away, but knowing him, he'd fucking chase me just for shits and giggles. Growing up in a small mountain town, you rely on your neighbors and have friends, or so-called friends, even if you don't want them.

"And here he is, folks, the mysterious grump from up the mountain," Robin announces, which would piss me off, but I hear Joey's sweet laughter even in this crowd. "Look at this sleek, shining beard, ladies. Let me hear your vote!"

Loud is fucking understatement; my ears split, and my head rattles. Women screech in high-pitched yells. To say I'm shocked wouldn't do this shit justice. I don't want to be up here, and I never would have given these women that impression, yet here I am displayed like a damn peacock.

I shake my head, about to make my way off stage, when the last thing I ever expect is shouted from the last woman I would expect it from.

"One hundred dollars!" Joey screams above all the cat calls.

"No!" I shout, pointing at her, but she just laughs, not remotely intimidated by me. Damn it.

"Two hundred!" A blonde in the front row says, shaking her money in the air.

This is my fucking nightmare.

"That's not how this works," I say, but no one can hear me. Especially not that deviant, Robin. The troublemaker bounces her eyebrows with mischief.

"Two hundred? Do we have Two-fifty for this handsome beard?"

"Three hundred!"

"Three fifty!"

"I'm not for sale, damn it," I growl, but thankfully, no one hears me over Joey.

"One thousand dollars!" She shouts, and Robin screams her enjoyment. With a wink, she announces the winner to be Joey. Thank god, and finally puts me out of my misery.

Stomping off stage, I've reached my people limit. The crowd parts for my large frame, except for a blonde that tries to stop me.

"Hey, I feel robbed." Her tone is flirty as she runs her long pink nails down my arm. "What are you doing after you finish your date with her? I would have paid more, you know."

"No thanks." I try to be respectful and step away, but she grabs my shirt pulling me closer. At the moment, I lock eyes with the woman I really want to be drawn to, and her face guts me. The confident smile she's been wearing all night falls, replaced by something I hate.

Hurt.

Without another thought, I plow forward, past the blonde who only falters a step, and straight to Joey. She's pulling her jacket back on, as some dick comes over to her.

"Fuck off," I growl just as he says hello.

Her eyebrows shoot to the sky, but she doesn't say anything as I take her hand and pull her to me.

"Let's get out of here." It's a rough command, but I need to get her alone. Everything about meeting her in person is messing with me, and if she's hurt, I'll fucking tear down the mountain to fix it.

She doesn't smile but nods, letting me take her hand. It's soft and so much smaller than mine. Her heat rises through my arm and makes me hard.

I take several deep breaths, hating the crowded room, wishing we were home instead of here. She just got here; I don't want to share her. Fuck, that's a bad sign.

At the door, I'm greeted by the town's new fireman, Trevor.

"Hey. It's Gavin, right? Can I buy you a beer and talk for a bit?"

I'm sure he wants to know about my flight schedule since I'm the only one who can fly in and out, but I don't have time.

"Not now."

"Oh, sure, no problem. Have a great night."

I grunt goodbye, and Joey waves politely.

"Nice to meet you, Trevor."

"You, too."

Finally, we make it to my truck. It's a bit chilly tonight, so I kick up the heat. Of course, she stares at me the entire drive home, expecting me to say something, the right thing.

The tension between us is at an all-time high, and I'm unsure if I can fight it. If she's against it, I'll back off and pray we can still be friends…but I got to shoot my shot.

BACK HOME, my truck jerks forward with the brakes, but I don't kill the engine. I let her purr and heat the cab as I work on the courage to tell her all the things I feel for her. That she's my sunshine in my darkest mood. My sole confidant and best friend, and yet so much more.

I take a deep breath and roll up my sleeve, exposing the blue butterfly tattoo on my wrist. Her warm touch follows a gasp as she scoots closer, taking off her seatbelt.

"Your tattoo is…"

"For you."

"Wow."

"Joey the only secret I haven't told you…" I don't get a chance to finish my sentence as she presses her lips to mine. Her fingers trail into my hair as she pulls my mouth harder against hers. Her lips are so soft I groan. Entranced in the best kiss of my life, the world could stop spinning, and I wouldn't care. Nothing could stop us from this moment. Were we always destined for this?

All I know is her mouth on me. My hands welcome her body as she straddles my lap. Taking control, she plunges her tongue into my mouth, deepening our kiss and, with it, our connection.

I grab hold of her moving hips, pressing her against my throbbing cock. Her moan is beautiful, and oxygen to my lungs. I buck for her. Grinding our needy parts in unison, longing for more.

"Take me inside, Gavin, but don't stop."

I growl at her request. The line between our friendship and more officially crossed. No going back now. Leaning forward, I take my key out and shoulder the door open, but I never stop kissing her. With her still wrapped around me, I walk us into the cabin. In my arms, she holds on, kissing my neck and running her fingers through my hair and beard. I light a quick fire at the push of a button and lay us across the large rug in front of the fireplace.

The room is painted in shadows that dance with every flicker of the fire. Looking down at her, so beautiful and vulnerable for me, my heart pumps faster.

"Joey, the only secret I've ever kept from you is you. You're the one person in my life I care for above anyone else, and I thought keeping the line between us would keep me safe, but fuck baby, this feels so much better."

She smiles, biting her lip.

"I didn't realize that, and now I feel like a hypocrite for being mad. I thought it was something you needed to talk about, and you were being all Gavin and keeping something painful locked up."

"Hypocrite? Joey, do you have a secret you're keeping from me?"

She nods with a light laugh.

"I've had the biggest crush on you. And all this sweet vulnerability you're showing me is making it very hard not to attack you, so I'm glad you feel the same way."

Suddenly she looks worried, and her smile is gone. "What?"

"You do want me? Like, do you see me as a woman and not as one of the guys? Not just your friend."

It's a statement, not a question. Like she can't believe it.

I'll put that insecurity to rest real fast. I thrust my hard erection against her warm heat.

"You are the most beautiful woman I've ever met. Never wanted anyone the way I want you, and I promise you it's not because of anything you wear but the sexy as hell woman you are on the inside. Your caring heart, your sassy fuckin' mouth, and that ass, my god." I make a show of biting my knuckle to make her laugh. It lifts boulders off my shoulders I didn't realize I was carrying. Then our bodies can't hold back anymore. Our lips crash hard, mine eager to devour her.

CHAPTER NINE

Joey

Our confessions seal our fate. Whether this growing relationship between us can last is debatable if we can't communicate off paper, but for the moment, I'm soaking up his affection. His mouth trails my neck, making me delirious with need. I've never felt like this before. Sexy and desired, but he makes it feel natural. Gavin's beard is a surprising contrast against my skin. It's soft but scratches along my skin, giving way to goosebumps.

I fumble with the buttons on his shirt, nervous that my lack of experience will turn him off. When he sits up and rips his shirt the rest of the way, buttons fly across the room, but his eyes stay laser-focused, burning into me. I can't help moaning at the dark hair that peppers his wide chest and trails down his pants. He's fit and muscular but so burly and thick. He easily covers my whole body with his when he lays back down.

Oh god, even his chest hair is soft. I rub against him, wanting more but too scared to ask for it.

"I'll shave, I promise."

I freeze at the thought. "No!"

He laughs, liking my answer.

"No, don't! You're so soft and rough and everything, god Gavin, I need you," I admit, no longer able to keep my composure as he grips my hip, the other hand gently playing in my hair and keeping his body from crushing me. The thought is enticing. At my greedy confession, he turns into an animal. Growling in my ear as he helps me out of my top. It's thrown off somewhere the light doesn't reach, followed by my fancy bra, pants, and undies.

Soon I'm on display under him, but instead of feeling scrutinized, I feel like a meal. The dark storm in his eyes lets me know exactly what I look like to him and gives me the courage to be daring to do something I really want to do. Sitting up, I push him back to sit on his ankles, and I adjust so I can comfortably take his belt off. Then I unbutton his jeans, and he rises enough to push them down, but I stop him from standing when I slide my hand inside his boxer briefs.

The growl he gives me makes me feel like a porn star. Like maybe I can make him feel good and not fumble. I lean down without another thought and take him in my mouth. He curses as I lean further in. Sucking and tasting him, coating him with my wet mouth, and groaning at the taste. This isn't something I've ever had the guts to do, but I know I'm safe with him, and with that thought, I reward my best friend for always making me feel like a better woman. For empowering me to take what I want and enjoying every second. His cock is so wide I'm scared I'll gag or, worse, get sick on him, but his sweet precum helps me work him down deeper. Keeping my hand on the base, I suck and pull and listen to his moans of pleasure. He can't hold still, and I don't want him to.

Gavin takes control, gently cupping the back of my head. I look up at him while I worship at his lap. Our eye contact is all the confirmation he needs to drive his dick faster and faster. Soon his sounds become too much, and if he doesn't come, I will.

"Fuck no," he mumbles, pulling back and releasing me.

"What's wrong?" Normally I would be scared I messed up, but this is Gavin, and I can just ask.

"I'm not coming in your mouth the first time I have you. No fucking way."

My excitement grows with his husky voice, but he stands, leaving me cold on the floor. He quickly pushes out of his pants and reaches in his wallet before returning. Then it's a hot, sweaty blur of body parts and years of fantasies being unleashed.

I lick my lips, still tasting him as he sheaths himself, but he doesn't line up. He kneels at my feet, placing a kiss on my foot, my ankle, fuck, why is he torturing me? Fire burns in my center as his wet mouth trails up my leg and across my inner thighs, teasing me. Nips from his teeth make me yelp, and I laugh at myself, enjoying it but wanting more.

"You want me to lick you, baby?"

"Fuck yes, please."

Oh my god, I never thought I would like dirty talk, but his grumbling voice raises my temperature.

His tongue slides across my panty line, and I gasp. So close yet still not where I need him. He repeats the action up the other side, then when he finally tastes me, we both moan in unison. His rich husky vibration causes my body to grab onto him for support. My fingers grip his sleek black hair as he laps up my slit, paying special attention to my clit. Flicking and sucking, I can't help but buck into his face.

Riding that fucking beard like it is my job. The sight is straight out of a porno, and in seconds, I'm shaking under his relentless mouth as he plunges his tongue inside me. It's so intense it almost hurts, but I don't want it to ever stop. He watches me gasp for air as I release my hold on him and melt into the soft rug under me. His mouth never stops, even as I catch my breath. Trailing lazy kisses up my pelvic bone and climbing up to look down at me. It's warm and comforting after something so earth-shattering.

"Are you ok?"

"Yes." My answer is no more than a blissful sigh.

"Have you ever, um…" he trails off, but I realize he thinks I'm a virgin. He's not far off.

"I have done this before, yes, one time."

Expecting my nerves that don't come, he rubs my cheek to let me know he cares.

"We can still stop if you want to."

"I don't want to stop. Ever." I admit, and I know it's too much, but it doesn't faze him. His lush mouth finds mine, with my lingering taste still on his tongue. It feels filthy and exhilarating, and as he makes love to my mouth, that need builds again.

"I want you, Gavin. I want you to fuck me. Make me feel you deep and hard and not like your friend."

"We are way past friends."

His purr is the last thing I hear before I scream, clutching onto his shoulders as he buries himself inside me. Slowly at first, but fuck, he is so thick I'm stretched to the max. When he fills me completely, he stops, but I can't; my hips beg him to move as I stay speechless, tears stinging my eyes, my body in pure euphoria. No competition, Gavin is fucking gold in bed, and I scream my praise for him to know it.

"Oh god, yes! Un-fucking-believable! My god, you're unreal! So good." I whimper as my climax builds again.

My words spur him on, and his thrust is so hard it jerks my body up the rug. His eyes watch my chest as my breasts bounce, and I grin, twist the rug in my fist, and push back into each punishing thrust of his hips.

"Fuck yes! Baby, take my cock. Take every fucking inch while you smile at me like that."

I do, clenching around him. In one graceful motion, he takes my legs over my shoulders, and with my hips, in his skillful hands, he pumps so hard and fast I'm lit up like a firework. Our voices rise with the awaiting tide, and I watch his cock pump inside me, glistening with my arousal; he's like a work of art. Gavin is a skilled machine with cords of muscle that strain to keep me close. Our sounds are filthy, sweat coating our bodies as he slaps against the back of my thighs. His deep growls sound agonizing.

"Harder!" I can't believe my own voice as I beg for more. "I'm so close!"

My body jerks with the force of his desire. He lets my legs fall around his sides to keep me close, and his mouth comes around my nipple. His wet tongue flicks, and I arch into him. The pleasure is blinding, and my eyes flutter closed.

"Come for me. Let me see you come for me."

I erupt at his command, overwhelmed with sensations. Ripples of pleasure seem to cascade through me in waves, from inside out.

He grunts with one last stroke before his own orgasm rocks him.

Slowly he pulls back, slips out, and rolls over, bringing me to rest on his chest.

I try to stay awake, not wanting this feeling to end, but soon, the steady beat of his heart under my ear takes me under.

CHAPTER TEN

Gavin

The sight of her eyes rolling back and mouth parted as she climaxed around me will forever be the greatest thing I have ever seen and will be permanently burned into my memory. I'm not even mad at my morning wood today. I embrace it, but rolling over, I only feel cold sheets. My eyes snap open as fear grips my lungs in a vice-like grip. I jump out of bed and hurry downstairs, instantly relieved when I hear her sweet voice whispering.

It's hard to make out.

Is she baby talking?

A few more steps, and I make it around the corner to find her on the couch with Billy the Kid, flipping through some of my old Rolling Stones magazines.

"If Axl Rose were to roll up in a limo with three anxiously awaiting lady goats, would you go, or would you rather be deserted on a desert island with Ozzy Osborne and a dozen super model goats?"

The Pygmy goat bleats his reply that she somehow understands, nodding her head.

"Me too."

"What are you doing out here?"

I laugh when she startles.

"Sorry."

"You should be." Her voice trails off as her eyes wander down my naked body. I don't bother to act bashful now; instead, I scoop her into my arms.

"I want you in my bed. Is that ok with you?"

"Yeah." She nods and kisses me as I walk us back. Bleats of disagreement sound behind us, but thankfully Billy the Kid stays put on the couch.

The next few hours are filled with moans and tangled sheets. We make love, slow and gentle, but then we fuck like animals and put a hole in my wall. It's all blurring, and as sudden as it is, knowing her through letters all these years makes it feel like we're old lovers. Sharing more than our bodies, but my heart, too. Part of me knows I gave it to her back when we were just kids. Innocent friends, but she was kind and understanding to a kid who struggled with emotions. She was my best friend and felt like my only ally. And now she was mine.

***

The morning is blissful, but eventually, we make our way out of the bedroom in need of sustenance.

"Eggs, ok?"

"You can never go wrong with eggs," Joey says, her hair a mess of tangles and her face clear of the makeup she wore last night. More beautiful now, lips still red from bearded kisses.

I love this girl. She's so raw and straight to the point. Knows exactly who she is even though sometimes she thinks it isn't enough. That's my job, though, to make sure she's never insecure again.

"After breakfast, I'd like to take you somewhere."

"Ok, I'm in."

I smile at my ride-or-die. The one person in this world who knows me the best. All my flaws and still came all this way for me. No questions asked; she'd go anywhere with me.

"Want to fly?"

"Yes!" She exclaims, that beautiful face lighting up with excitement. "Mind if I go shower off all your love juices."

I laugh.

"I mean, you know." She blushes, turning away from me.

"Yeah, I really do know what you mean."

My admission is thick in my throat. I can't tell her I love her yet. It's only been a fucking day. Years of friendship led us to this time in our lives, and I have to believe it's finally our time. That we can make this work. So I keep the raw words inside as I watch her nod solemnly. Maybe she knows. Joey can see things in me I can't, and this one time, I hope she can read between the lines. Although if she doesn't feel as deeply as I'm feeling yet, that's ok too. As long as I can keep her here with me, I have to hope she'll love me back one day.

Eggs and bacon eaten, showered, and Billy the Kid safely secured, we take the Four Wheeler out to the garage. I love her gasp when I pull open the large bay doors and show off the collection of birds my grandad, and I have bought over the years.

"Wow. Impressive."

I lazily find the keys to the new Kodiak, just wanting to watch her face as she takes in my life's work. This isn't something I've ever shared with anyone but Grandad, and I think he would have approved of Joey. Aside from being sexy as hell, she's capable. Knows and understands the tools on the walls. I stand in awe of her as she steps up and peeks into the open hood of Billy Jean. What I thought was fixed isn't, and she won't fly anymore, so I just left the hood off. After the last shaky flight, I've come to terms it might have been her last.

"You're giving up on her?"

"Not exactly, but she probably won't fly safely again."

"I think she can." Her voice trails off as she struts around the old beast.

The hope in her voice is all I need to reaffirm my love for this woman.

"She's old. Might need to donate her to a museum at this point."

Standing back and wiping her hands on her jeans, she just shrugs. "Maybe, but if it's all the same to you when we get back, I'd like to take a look."

"Of course, it's fine with me. What's mine is yours if you'll stay."

"I told you I would stay. Are you scared I'll leave? You like me that much, huh?"

Her eyes search mine. Maybe I'm wrong, and she wants to hear me say it out loud.

I don't, though. I clear my throat and point to the shiny new plane my clients expect to be chaperoned in. Might not have in-flight snacks, but if they're willing to pay my big price tag, I'll haul whatever they want almost anywhere.

"Yeah, I like you, all right." It slips out as she turns to get into the cockpit, giving me a view of that thick ass of hers. The memories of how she feels make me growl, but she likes it. Laughing with flushed cheeks and a knowing look in her eyes.

I hurry to my side and get settled in, starting her up. Driving the bird out of the hanger and onto the strip like I have a million times before suddenly feels different with such precious cargo.

At takeoff, she bursts into a giddy laugh. She's never flown before. She had never been out of her little town, and she took a big leap to come to me, so I'm going to do everything in my power to show her the world. Call me fucking Aladdin, and I'll take her on as many magic carpet rides as she wants. Show her mountains, then the sea. Islands both hot and cold, so she can decide which she likes better. This is just the start of our adventure. The fun has only just begun.

CHAPTER ELEVEN

Joey

A thrill runs up my spine as we lean into sharp mountain peaks soaring around them and between rocky ridges. We've been up here for an hour, and I know we'll have to touch back down to earth sooner rather than later, but I still don't want it to stop.

"Close your eyes for me."

I'm surprised by his request, and as much as I don't want to obey because I'm having so much fun, I do as I'm told. Knowing Gavin will reward me. The pressure in the plane changes, and I'm glad to be wearing headphones, so I don't have to suffer a headache.

"Now open."

Again, I obey his command, and when I open my eyes, a large flowing waterfall comes into view, beating down to the earth below. It's twenty times the size of the one by his house. The scene is breathtaking, and I take it all in silently, in awe.

Wildflowers grow in the moss that covers the rocky boulders below, and rushing water streams down the mountainside. Dark reds, oranges, and yellows paint the trees for autumn.

"It's like something from a story," I shout into the headset, my ears ringing with the vibration of the small plane.

A sudden jerk scares me, and suddenly we're nose-diving. A yelp escapes me; even though I trust Gavin completely, knowing he's been flying his whole life, I'm stuck between fear and excitement. I heady mix as the sexy pilot beside me takes control, maneuvering us close to the water but not close enough to be in any danger.

"I got you."

"I know! I trust you," I reply.

The plane shakes almost violently as he strategically lands in a long empty field. When the wheels hit the ground, it's bumpy but not out of control. No, Gavin has full control and safely brings us to a stop.

As soon as he gives me that cocky grin, I know we're good to go, so I jump out of the seatbelt, excited to take in such a beautiful place.

The sound of the chirping birds and splashing water is the first thing I notice. The second is Gavin's powerful presence. At the water's edge, he wraps his arms around me in an embrace I feel all the way to my toes. I want to spill all the words of love, longing, and adoration to him, but he wants me to stay, and for now, that's good enough.

Wanting a man who doesn't communicate well could break my heart. I trust Gavin more than anyone on this planet, and if I lose him because I rushed him, I'll never forgive myself. He needs me as much as I need him; coming here has proved that. We're great together. Gone are my former insecurities about whether he would see me as feminine. There is no question of his desire for me. Proving my point, his thick erection grinds into my backside, and I moan shamelessly pushing back into him.

"Fiend."

I gasp at the hypocrisy.

"You're one to talk, Mr. I want you in my bed. You're the one pressing into me here."

"Oh, I know, I'm worse. I just wanted you to know I like it."

I laugh as he takes my hand, leading me closer to the waterfall. The sun is hot and bright today, but I imagine the spring water will be freezing.

"Want to go for a swim?"

"In that? Isn't it cold?"

"Yes," he says, pulling his long flannel off his shoulders and tossing it to the mossy rocks nearby and kicking off his shoes, followed by his pants. He's really going in. Well, ok then, we're going swimming. I swear this man leads me on a new adventure every day.

I take a deep breath and shed my clothes as he splashes into the wading dark water. We're perfectly secluded out here, and something about being naked in the wild is exhilarating. Placing a timid toe into the cold water, I whine at the confirmation. The sitting water of the pond here is probably in the chilly forty degrees or lower.

"This is not what I thought you had in mind for today."

"Oh, come on now, ride-or-die. The more things you try out, the more you know what you like and what you want."

I hum at the nickname, thinking about all the words not said. All the things I could fill in. Thoroughly enticed, I force myself to plow through and dive in. Coming up for air, I gasp in shock. Even knowing the water would be cold couldn't prepare me, but just as quickly, I'm engulfed by a warm body with rippling muscles and that scruffy beard. Wrapping around him, I hold on, unable to touch the bottom, but he can and steadies us. We don't say anything for a moment, just take it all in.

Out here in the middle of nowhere, it's so peaceful. No sounds of traffic or endless people chattering. It's just us, at one with nature and each other. For so long, I thought I wouldn't be able to have this. A connection with someone who really gets me. A man who sees me under the hood of a machine and actually has fire in his eyes. Gavin doesn't treat me like one of the guys, yet I can joke around and not be girly or perfect. Hell, I've burped in front of the man a handful of times already. He wants me to stay. I don't have to be anything but myself with him, and my heart soars at the possibility of our future together.

We're only a few inches from the crashing falls now, and it's all I can hear. Our bodies are pressed so tightly to each other that it's becoming hard to take in the scenery or think of anything else. Gavin is all I can feel. His rough chest hair rubs against my sensitive nipples, and I bite my lip. How much sex can someone have before they hurt themselves? The two of us have been insatiable; still, my body and heart want more.

His lips find my ear, but I get a hell of a lot more than the kiss I expect.

"You make me happy, Joey Bennett."

My chest fills with so much emotion I almost choke. Coming here was the right decision. Not just for him. I needed this change, and it gave me a chance to explore this new me. A small town girl lost in the throes of love in the wilderness.

Afraid I'll confess my love too early, I seal my mouth to his. Kissing him with all the happiness he's filled me with.

Hoping he knows how amazing I think he is. Knowing that our future is so bright.

The kiss soon becomes more, and his wet mouth and soft beard move to my sensitive neck, eliciting a moan. God, I love his beard. Our bodies wade closer, his rigid muscles pressing against my soft curves. Soon I'm wrapped around his waist and grinding myself shamelessly against him. I gasp when his crown rubs against me. The freezing temperature is long forgotten as Gavin heats me up from the inside.

"I want to take you here, now, but if you don't, just say the word." His words are heavy and laced with desire as his eyes burn into mine.

"Yes, now."

"God, yes," he grits through his teeth. In one slow thrust of his hips, he enters me, stretching me completely, and I can't help but scream from the intense pleasure.

"That's it. Take all of me like a good girl. Scream as loud as you want, baby; it fucking fuels me."

I moan out his name as he impales me on his massive cock, and holy hell, it's the most earth-shattering experience. The cold water splashes around us, and our slick bodies slide, but he controls me, gripping my thighs with unforgiving hands.

"Harder!" I demand, so close to the edge already.

"You better fucking hold on then."

I grip his hair in two fists as my arms wind tighter around his shoulders, and I bite down on his shoulder, loving the screams I entice.

His girth stretches me, and his powerful thrusts are so relentlessly I'm afraid he might split me in two. The thought only turns me hotter. I scream, taking each punishing thrust. Water splashes around us as our bodies make a wave pool. Making filthy sounds that drive us higher.

"You're going to come for me. You're going to quake on my fat cock as if it were your wildest adventure."

"Oh, Gavin, fuck yes!"

His hips drive impossibly deeper inside me as he growls in my ear. The husky words claw inside me as deep as his cock.

"I'll fill you with everything I have because I want you to have it all."

Those pounding hips rut against me, his cock still driving me to the peak of something bigger than I've ever felt. His lower abdomen strikes my clit, again and again, and I'm crashing into the waves around me, and he's falling too. Our moan is loud and in rhythm with each other. My orgasm grips around his swelling cock, but he only slows his movement. Drawing out each intense wave of pleasure until I'm putty in his hands, and he's kissing me softly and holding me close while we catch our breath.

The moment is surreal. Our bodies were meant for each other, and with all my heart, I hope we are too. That we can build a life together filled with adventures like this. If not, I'm officially ruined for anyone else. No one will ever compare to this man who holds so much more than my body in this moment.

CHAPTER TWELVE

Gavin

Weeks go by, and Joey and I fall into an easy routine together. Up with the sun most days, only to stay in bed making love for an extra hour or so. Then we head out, feed Billy the Kid, and work on Billy Jean. She's almost back to her former glory, and I haven't told Joey yet, but I have a museum interested in buying her, and the money would be a big enough chunk of change to finally take one of the big trips we always talked about.

"I could show you the world."

She giggles, not entirely aware of my plan.

"Take me wonder by wonder?"

I hum with a smile as we reach my truck, parked right next to her car, which still has the same flat tire. We could both easily change it. I could have changed it instead of paying a very reluctant Vance Owen to tow it up here. Not his job indeed, but I thanked him with a bottle of Jack, and he seemed to understand. I don't know why I'm still scared she'll leave. It's just hard feeling so much for someone like my heart just walking around outside my chest all day.

"I will, you know. Got big plans for it, in fact."

"Oh, do tell me all about these magical lands." Her tone is flirty, and my eyes can't help but wander down her neck. Getting a peek at her ample chest, I growl with satisfaction. I am one lucky son of a bitch. Gripping her thigh like I've become accustomed to doing lately, I shake my head.

"Secret."

"Oh, that's not fair. You can't just tell me there's something exciting but not actually tell me what it is…that's just mean, Gavin."

I smile but don't give in. Instead, I keep my eyes on the road ahead. We're going into town for lunch at Pour Decisions. Joey and Robin are thick as thieves these days. Sure didn't take my town long to fall for her as hard as I have.

Every weekend we come for a late beer but no more sharing. Joey made it clear she was thankful and paid my bill, but if Robin tried to pull me into another auction of man meat, she wouldn't be sharing and didn't care if she broke the bar down fighting for me. Someone could have offered me the jet plane from Top Gun; still, I wouldn't have felt as good as I did hearing her say that. She fucking loves me. I can feel it in every small touch of my bicep. She always tries to make me something to eat even though she sucks at cooking anything. When she gets dirty under the hood of one of my planes and actually asks questions even though part of me thinks she knows the answer. Joey gets me. She knows I love talking nuts and bolts and lets me gush over the fact. And I reward her generously. Whether in my bed or at a waterfall, I'm far from done when it comes to spoiling her.

Pulling into the small parking lot on the side of the building, we make our way inside. Robin greets us with a wave, and we take our usual stools at the bar.

"Roast beef," I say, not bothering to open the lunch menu.

"Same."

Robin just laughs at us. Another thing Joey and I have in common is our simple taste in food.

"Oh, you two are a match made in heaven, aren't ya."

We don't respond, but a small smile that matches mine shines on her face.

"Sure gonna miss seeing y'all's happily ever after."

"What? Where are you going?" Joey's attention snaps to Robin. This is news to both of us.

"I need a change, so I'm selling the bar and moving down to the Keys for some much-needed sun and sand. Trading barflies for Mai Tai's, babe."

"We have those things," I grumble because, honestly, I hate to see her leave. Robin is one of the few people in this town that I like. A proper owner of a rowdy bar that never gets out of hand. That kind of power over your people comes naturally to her, and I can't think of anyone else who could replace her.

"Right, but since this is the only small town I've ever seen, I'm taking a lesson from your fearless pen pal here and taking an adventure of my own."

Well, damn, when she puts it that way, I can't blame her. Is there anyone who just wants to stay in one place forever? Surely the people of my town who were born and raised aren't miserable, are they? Maybe I should do some pro-bono flights just for fun. With the money for Billy Jean, I could make that happen.

"But, you're my only friend." Joey whines.

I grunt at her words even though I'm not really offended.

"You don't count," she says, her face softening, and Robin laughs. I know what she means. I'm not just her friend, and she's not mine, although she is still my best friend, and I know I'm hers. We haven't lost anything between us but gained so much more, like orgasms.

"You can fly down and see me. I just can't sit here hoping to meet Mr. Right when Mr. Billy Bob and his missing teeth is the only one in this town showing me any interest. Now I'm ok not being someone's cup of tea, but I know all the men in this town and the tourists are losing their appeal. I need a change and a real bonafide date. Dinner and drinks, a movie maybe. Fuck, do guys still gift flowers? I'd love a man to give me flowers."

Just then, a man in the back eating at a booth belches, and Robin sighs, putting up a hand as if to say, see my point.

"I rest my case."

"Ok. For the record, I hate the idea and everything about it, but I just did the same thing, and it's the best decision I ever made, so go, fly away, little birdie." Joey moves her fingers as if to release Robin into the wild, if not reluctantly. "But wait, who'll run this place?"

"I don't know. Honestly, the board of tourism would love to see me close. Tear down this eye sore, maybe put in a Margaritaville."

"No," I grumble at the thought.

"Well, it's going up for sale on the first, whether we all like it or not."

Joey groans her unhappiness. "Well, I'm happy for you, if I have to be."

The girls laugh, but I worry with her friend gone, will I be enough to keep Joey happy in Sycamore Mountain? She tells me she loves it here, but it's not even been a month. If all she has is me…will I be enough?

CHAPTER THIRTEEN

Joey

I don't know what it is about mornings, but I love this time of day. Gavin is a natural early riser and this morning is no different. Before my eyes even have a chance to open, his mouth is on me. That lush beard tickles the insides of my legs as he moves over me. Still naked from the night before, he finds his meal easily, and with the first lick of his wide tongue, I'm wide awake. I moan with the intense sensation he causes. Each delicious flick he delivers with expert precision and relentlessly devours my most intimate place. I arch and thrash under his power. Calling his name, moaning as he brings me to the peak, I crash hard, shaking with a blissful orgasm. Slowly he licks his way up and kisses my hip bone.

"God baby, you taste so good."

"You are unbelievable. Had I known you would be

addicted to my lady taco, I would have moved out here long ago."

He laughs and hops out of bed.

"Where are you going? We aren't done."

"God knows it pains me to deny you anything, but I have a flight. I've got to go get a client and bring him back to his cabin here with his old lady. I'd love for you to come, but I really have to watch my weight."

He brings me a warm wet washcloth, and instead of giving it to me, he runs it gently across my sensitive center. Gently but with ownership. His eyes burn for me, and still, he doesn't make a move to take more. My heart might actually explode if he keeps this up.

"Are you saying I weigh so much I would bring your plane down?" I joke, but his face is priceless.

"No. Of course fucking not." He shakes his head frantically. "I would never. It's just the max capacity, and with four people, I was just worried about the luggage they might be bringing, which I can't account for before take-off. But baby, if you want to come, I'll tell them if they want the ride, they can't bring shit. Please come."

After a long pause, he growls as I slowly grin an evil smile to let him know I was joking with him.

"You're a brat."

"You should spank me then."

Another husky growl, and he steps back and closes his eyes.

"I can't. If I don't get going, I won't be back in time to cook dinner for you. You'll starve. They don't deliver pizza up here."

I gasp.

"Go! Get out! Right now, shoo!"

He continues to laugh as I force him into the shower.

"Okay, okay, I'm goin'."

When he turns the water on, I slip into his boxers and a big t-shirt and make my way into the kitchen. Maybe I could make him a sandwich to take. I can't burn a turkey sandwich.

Billy the Kid greets me with his adorable bleats, kicking and jumping, so I take a moment to pet and feed him. The little guy has wormed his way into my heart as much as Gavin has. Living in the mountains is a lot different than back home, but I love it. Even the view is better. Instead of rolling waves washing in, I get rolling mountains covered in pine trees as far as the eye can see. They're beginning to change into beautiful fall colors, making me want to grab the smutty romance novel Octavia gave me and sit by the window.

Instead, I make quick work of packing a lunch I hope he doesn't hate and fill a thermos of hot black coffee. When he comes out smelling like the wild musky mountain man he is, I have a very hard time letting him go.

"But you're going to hurry back, right? And you'll be safe?"

"I've flown this exact route for Vince and his girl Harper a dozen times now. Don't worry. As soon as I land, I'll call you. Show you the wild city of San Francisco, so you'll cross it off your list and not make me go there."

My laugh is weak. He's trying to cheer me up, but I've never been up here alone, and I'm going to miss him.

"I'll miss you," Gavin says, placing a small kiss on my nose. The man even reads minds now.

"I'll miss you more."

Just for fun, I rub his jeans until I get that growl I love so much.

"Bye."

"Bye," I reply when he finally pulls away and makes his way to the newer Kodiak he uses for personal flights. It's sleek and offers more comfort than the other planes he mostly flies for cargo.

He works fast, and too soon, I'm waving goodbye to the bird in the air as the man I've fallen in love with flies out of sight.

The rest of the morning moves fast as I finish the final touches on Billy Jean, Gavin's grandpa's first plane. The old baddie was beat up and bruised, but Gavin and I got her running, and with this last coat of paint, she'll shine like the first day he saw her. A big part of me wants this to give him closure. To have something special of his grandpa's and be able to move forward. He's opened up to me more outside of our letters, but he's still stoic and unfriendly when we go to town. When Robin told us she was moving yesterday at lunch, he clammed up completely.

"What do you think?" I ask my plucky little sidekick, who bleats a few times, and I nod my understanding.

"You're right. It needs something a little more…. sentimental."

Suddenly my goat friend takes off toward the office.

"Hey! Wait a minute. Do you know something I don't?" I shout pointlessly as I follow Billy the Kid into the room he disappeared into.

It's not Gavin's office but his grandpa's; by the looks of things, it hasn't been touched in a long time. It's dusty, and stacks of boxes and engine parts lay scattered. I take a deep breath at his desk and sit in his chair.

"Whoa," I whisper to no one. Feeling the old man's presence even though I know he's not here. It's been over a year, and a dusty glass of bourbon sits atop a stack of papers as if he drank it just last night. For a moment, I wonder if he has a picture of him and Gavin somewhere. Bonus points if it's next to the old Billy Jean. The thought has me rummaging through the rickety brown desk.

Flight records? No, that's lame.

"Aww, look Billy, it's you."

I turn the photo of Billy the Kid in Gavin's arms for the pygmy goat to see. He humors me with a trot of excitement.

"This is defiantly going on our fridge."

I freeze at my own words. *Our fridge.*

It certainly feels like *our* home, but we never had the moving in with each other talk. He says things like he wants me to stay, but there are no plans for the future. As a matter of fact, we haven't even been on an official date aside from drinks at the bar, and he's never referred to me as his girlfriend. Gavin is a man of little words, but his actions tell me not to worry. That he wants me. What if he doesn't want a commitment long term?

No, he would never risk our friendship to just hook up. We've been friends too long for him to jeopardize that. Gavin wouldn't hurt me.

That was my last thought before I noticed my name on the envelope under the glass of bourbon.

CHAPTER FOURTEEN

Joey

ears blur my vision as I race down the mountain.
Gavin's words still haunt me.
You know you let people walk all over you, don't you?
This is dumb. We aren't kids anymore.

Every toxic comment he wrote me. Five fucking pages explaining to me all the reasons he didn't want to write to me anymore. He didn't put our friendship above everything else like I had. Gavin's letter made me realize I've been living in a fantasy. One that felt too good to be true because it was. I was never meant to move here or meet him. I should have stayed home, received that letter, and moved on from my stupid crush. Instead, he showed me all the things I wanted to see, knowing damn well he didn't plan on me staying.

The drive down the mountain is steep and narrow, and I honestly don't know if I'm going the right way. Hiccups hit me hard, and I shake with a broken heart. Billy the Kid is on the floor bleating for me to stop, but my head is so clouded I don't hear it as the warning to slow down, and I cut the corner too quick, then suddenly I'm plowing into the bumper of a pickup truck. The tires of my old car skid across the gravel, and my heart lurches as my car doesn't stop; instead, it leans too far over the side. Gravity pulls me closer to the rocky cliff. I scream in fear as my trunk tips over the edge. There we sit. Billy is now in my lap, me holding him tight, begging him not to move us off balance.

I'm a blubbering mess, too afraid to move but screaming for help as I white knuckle my steering wheel and squeeze my goat so tight I hope the poor thing can still breathe. Just when I feel the car shift, I send up one last prayer to God to save us, then suddenly, my door swings open, and two large arms rip me out.

Me and my goat land hard on our hero, and when I glance back just in time to watch all my belongings tumble down the cliff. A huge boom sounds around us as trees break, and the crunch of metal sounds through the trees. Then finally, the old beater meets her death at the gruesome bottom of the mountain.

Righting ourselves, the man clears his throat, and I notice another man with a nice smile and an outstretched hand which I take and get to my feet.

"Oh my god, thank you." It is all I can manage. My tears have stopped, but that's because of the shock and panic currently taking over. I almost fell down the mountain. I just lost everything.

"Hey, now, it's alright. You're alright. I'm Ajax Grayson, and this is my brother. Everything's going to be alright."

"It's really not," I whisper but then snap out of it. These guys just saved my life. "I mean, thank you. You saved us. Thank you so much."

"Well, sure. What are you doing out here? Can we take you home?"

Emotion blocks my throat. I don't belong here, and yet this stupid mountain is trying to keep me…or kill me.

"Could I get a ride into town? I'm friends with Robin at Pour Decisions. I can use her phone to call…"

I don't want to admit it, but I want to call my daddy. Fuck, this hurts so much, and his big bear hug is exactly where I want to be right now.

"Do you have someone to call, ma'am?"

"Yeah. A ride would be great, thanks."

The two handsome men in government-looking uniforms, rangers maybe, nod and lead a shaking Billy the Kid and me to their truck. Or maybe it's me that's shaking.

"I'm so sorry about your truck. I have full insurance and will be happy to take care of the repairs myself if you'd like… or well, I guess I could stay to repair it, or just pay for it," I say once buckled up in between the two burly mountain men.

"You a mechanic?" Ajax asks to my right.

"I am, yeah."

"You doin' some work for Gavin?"

I just nod, not wanting to get into details, and he must sense my hesitation because the conversation drops, and we continue down the steep drive down the mountain. Ajax stops and honks at each sharp turn, listening for a honk back before making the turn. If I had known to do that, I might be on the highway back to Starlight Bay. As it is, I'm stuck here until I can pay my debt and get a new car.

Twenty minutes later, we're pulling into the local dive bar. The guys won't leave my side, and they swear it's because they want to make sure I'm alright and it has nothing to do with the damage to their truck. If I were in the city, I wouldn't believe them, but these men seem very protective, and after the chaos of my day, it's nice to not feel alone.

"No goats, Joey," Robin says, wiping down the counter, but when she double-takes, her face is a mask of panic. "What happened? What's wrong?"

I break down crying, and she wraps me in her arms. We both squish Billy the Kid, but he doesn't make a peep.

"Why do you have a goat?"

"I'm stealing him," I sniffle.

"From who?"

"Gavin."

"Gavin had a goat?"

"Yeah. He's really wonderful if he lets you know him, but you always have to question how serious he is because he's so quiet. Then you find out he's not in as deep as you are, and it's all been physical, and you've only been with one other person, and now you're ruined and lost your best friend at the same time, and I don't want to go back home, Robin." My words are rushed and mixed with tears, but she nods as if she understands.

"You guys have whatever you want on the house. I'll be right back."

The Grayson brothers shake their heads. "No need, Robin, we just wanted to make sure she was safe. We'll be getting back up the mountain. Have a nice evening, ladies."

"I owe you guys so big. Robin, they saved our lives," I blubber, kissing the top of Billy's head.

She just smiles, waving goodbye to the men and leading me back to her office. The worn-out old blue couch has a mess of blankets.

"Did you sleep here?" I sniffle.

"Don't you go worrying about me now? Tell me what

happened, and if me and my shotgun need to have a heart-to-heart with your boyfriend."

"He's not my boyfriend," I shrug, settling into her blankets on the couch. Billy the Kid nuzzles into my armpit, not wanting to leave me, and my heart melts, needing all the affection I can get.

"What are you talking about? You guys have been inseparable since you came into town. Plus, I thought you guys were taking it to O-town like several times a day…"

"That's the thing. I found this long-ass letter, and Robin, it was like he saw through me. Like he's known how much I've loved him this whole time and used my secrets to hurt me. A part of me knows he's been hurting, and it could have been his way to take out his pain on me, and he never sent the letter, but fuck…I will not be anyone's punching bag."

"I'm so sorry, Joey. I don't know what exactly was in the letters, but I'm so sorry you had to read them."

"Then, as I was leaving, my Jeep went over the edge of the mountain after I hit the Graysons."

"Well fuck. I'm so glad you're alive!" She hugs me. Her spicy perfume fills my nose, comforting me. "This day can go suck a donkey dick. How about I grab some ice cream and root beer, and we spike our floats with whiskey and forget our troubles? I'll close up for the night, and you and me can just chill with your smelly goat friend."

I laugh, even though I want to defend Billy's smell. "Deal."

CHAPTER FIFTEEN

Gavin

Something was wrong. When I landed, I called Joey, but she didn't answer. Then I called her twenty more times until Vince and Harper were buckled and ready, and I couldn't delay anymore. Now I was struggling not to panic. What if she took the Four Wheeler out and flipped it, or something else equally as heart-wrenching happened? What if someone went up there and realized she was all alone?

Fuck.

My head is a mess, but I still have to get my clients home. Part of me has faith in my girl. Joey is strong and capable, and I trusted that when I left her, but a nagging feeling of dread looms at the forefront of my thoughts until I finally touch down on Sycamore Mountain.

She is here, my girl is here somewhere, and soon I'll be able to hold her. Everything is going to be fine.

But it isn't. Joey isn't here. Beside my truck is an empty space where her Jeep used to sit. Panic rises, and my gut squeezes with uncertainty. Too many what if's and worst-case scenarios flash through my mind. Once I am parked safely inside the garage, I cut the engine and then bolt to the house. Luckily Vince has an SUV waiting to take him to the other side of the mountain.

"Joey!" I yell, bursting through my front door. "Joey!"

No sign of her. All her bags are gone, and Billy the Kid is nowhere to be found.

She left. She willingly packed up her things and left. Was she unhappy? This morning when I left, we were solid. Why the fuck would she leave?

I knew I wasn't enough.

A scream rips through my chest, and I fall to my knees. My hands shake as the emptiness of the room starts to creep in. Depression is something I'm all too familiar with. Without her, why bother fighting it?

"Hey, buddy, are you ok?" Harper stands at the door frame with worry etched on her face.

"Fine," I pant. Still out of breath from screaming.

"I'm going to venture that you're not. I don't want to make it worse, but we wanted to let you know your office is a wreck. Papers are blowing out everywhere."

"What?"

Her words confuse me. My office is always closed. I hardly ever go in there because it still feels like my grandad's.

"Papers are flying out into the field. There seems to be a lot just scattered everywhere, I'm sorry I couldn't see much, but Vince pointed out they seem to be coming from your office. Should we close it for you?"

"No. Have a good night, Harper."

"Ok then. Thanks for the ride." She easily brushes off my cold demeanor and disappears into the waiting SUV. I make my way back to the garage. Sure, enough white pieces of paper swirl in a gust of wind and glide to my feet. More litter the ground. When I lean down to pick it up, I almost fall over. The first piece I pick up is a part of my hate letter to Joey. The one I wrote to hurt myself by pushing her away. The letter I couldn't bring myself to send because I knew the words would hurt her, and that's something I swore I'd never do.

This is why Joey's not here. She read the letter.

Fuck. My chest constricts, and I heave a heavy breath, weighed down by my mistake. Those pages should have been burned. They never should have stayed on this earth where she could find them.

The pain of my own betrayal burned in my gut. Falling to my knees is the only thing I can think to do. I hurt the only person on this earth that cared a fuck about me. Wanted all my bad, even when it was ugly. How did I repay that kindness by throwing every one of her insecurities in her face for the purpose of self-destruction? It worked. My heart was annihilated, and it felt a million times worse than when I wrote those lies.

The question is if I am going to do anything about it. Can I explain to Joey she was never meant to read it? It was all a lie. I was drunk and self-loathing.

Fuck no. It's not ok. Getting drunk and spewing my agony to hurt someone I care about is not ok. So even if she never forgives me, I have to make sure she's ok. That she knows she isn't her insecurities, but truly the greatest person I've ever met. She is everything. Joey Bennett is the smartest woman I know, capable of fixing anything she sets her mind to. Kind and compassionate even to small goats that eat her hair and shit in her shoes. She loves that little devil so much that she stole Billy the Kid. I couldn't even be mad. I love that about her.

And God, she is beautiful. Beyond compare, but I know she couldn't see it. Didn't understand the way her hips beg me to bite them. Or that her soft tan skin is my weakness. I longed to touch her constantly. If just to touch her hand or hug her to my chest. Those were the moments that churned in my mind as I picked myself up off the ground. I needed a plan. Action to keep me from a downward spiral. Something to show Joey that I love her and didn't mean anything I wrote. This needed to be big, but then again, Joey is simple and wouldn't fall for any grand gesture. It needed to be something that would show and tell her all the things I'd been struggling to voice.

With determination filling my lungs, I tossed the old glass of bourbon along with the letters into the firepit and torched it. Setting flame to my mistakes, I think about my Grandad.

"What advice would you have for me, old man?"

I'm sure he would say, don't bother. Women are too complicated, him having been divorced from my grandma my whole life. But with every pump of blood through my veins, I know I have to fight for her.

I loved the old man, but he was old and bitter and never once owned up to his mistakes. The realization hits hard. That my hero wasn't the greatest man, I always thought he was. In fact, he was a grumpy asshole just like me.

Joey deserves better. She deserves to hear how much she is loved, and I won't give up until I make sure she knows it. My heart be damned, I am going to tell her everything and pray she will forgive me. No matter how long it took. If we couldn't find a way back to each other after this, she would at least know how great she was.

Now for a plan.

CHAPTER SIXTEEN

Joey

"I'm never hanging out with you again," I groan in agony as Robin whistles.

"You love me."

"You're obnoxious."

She shrugs, not denying it, but she redeems herself with an outstretched cup of coffee.

"Oh, bless you. I do love you. You're a goddess."

Robin doesn't laugh, which is a bit suspicious, considering she lives for compliments.

"What is it?"

"What do you mean, what?"

"You're acting weirdly quiet. Did I do something stupid last night? I lost my phone, so it couldn't have been a drunk text confessing my unrealistic love for the man I'm furious with and yet still can't stop missing so much it hurts."

I laugh with no humor. My heart still pulling me up the

mountain where I really wanted to be this morning. Part of me closed my eyes last night and hoped it was all a bad dream and I'd wake up to the familiar husky snores of the bearded brute.

The saddest thing is I don't believe a word he wrote. I know in my bones he didn't mean any of it. No one, especially not a man, has ever cherished me the way Gavin has. Taken care of my well-being or bothered to look past my baggy clothes. Gavin made me believe in myself when I couldn't see myself as anything special.

"Ouch."

Billy the Kid pulls my hair, trying to take a bite…or get my attention. A letter sits beside my glass of water from the night before. The envelope is addressed to me but has no address and is unopened.

"What's this?"

"A letter from you know who," Robin says into her steaming mug.

"Gavin wrote me this? He's here?"

"He came by last night, and I sent him on his way because you were out cold, but this morning he showed up with coffee, and boo, I love ya, but we needed it, so I accepted. There are also donuts."

"Donuts?"

"Yep. Frosted ones."

"Damn, he's good."

He knew exactly how to penetrate my fortress and get past my gatekeeper. I find myself smiling for the first time since before I read the letter. My heart squeezes with the possibility of him fighting to apologize. I was worried he would spiral downward, leaving me to think he really felt those things he wrote about me. But again, actions speak louder than words, and Gavin has shown me so much love this last month, hell, since we were kids, that I had to hold onto some hope that he would come for me. That he would fight and not give up.

I want, no, need, for him to come out of his shell and show me that my feelings weren't one-sided. Fine, he's not a talker. He's a stubborn son of a bitch, but he loves me, and he's trying to show me. I can at least enjoy the sentiment. And I do; three chocolate-covered donuts later and coffee drunk, I shower and sit down at Robin's table to take a hard look at my life. What do I want? My things are currently at the bottom of a mountain, but I can't think of a single item I miss. I didn't even want my old ratty sweats anymore. Now that I know tighter jeans and tank tops with push-up bras make me feel sexy and confident, I don't want my old things. No, I needed a change.

"Here are some clothes."

"Oh gosh, thank you. You don't have to give me these."

"I know, but they suit you."

"Ripped jeans and a tattered old Tennessee whiskey shirt make you think of me."

"Mmm hmm, yep."

I laugh and change into the clothes. Truth be told, looking in the mirror makes me feel more like the Joey I wanted to be. Strong, chin tipped up. The cleavage is on point. I am going to make the life I always wanted, and damn it, I'm not going to let a man chase me from a place I don't want to leave.

"Sell me the bar," I blurt out without an extra thought.

"You want…? What?"

"Let me buy you out of Pour Decisions. I don't want to leave Sycamore Mountain, but I'm sure as hell not staying for a man I'm currently mad at. Now, I do want that grumpy idiot, but he has a lot to prove, and I can't just move back up there and let him take care of me anymore. I've been under a man's thumb, whether it was my dad or my brother, my whole life. I need something for me, and what better than buying the bar I love?"

"Um, wow, ok then. Consider it yours. You got the money? Or do you want to head over to the bank?"

"I think I can swing it. Life savings come in handy when you want to start all over."

"Ok, then."

With that settled, a new purpose flows through my veins. Excitement I had never felt before courses through me, and I hope it would all be for the best. That this huge life decision I made a month ago led me here for a reason, and my happiness isn't just pinned on Gavin. That's too much to put on one person, and I won't. It's not fair. I need to go out and make my own way, starting with this bar.

CHAPTER SEVENTEEN

The Letter

Dear Joey,

When I was eight, you told me if I was a stupid boy and stopped being your pen pal because you were a girl, you'd come to find me someday and punch me in the nose. I deserve that hit more than ever now. I know I hurt you with the letter you found, but God, Joey, you have to know me well enough to know I didn't mean a single word.

I promised myself this wouldn't be some half ass letter with a dozen excuses, so I'll tell you honestly, I let myself crawl into a depression where I hated myself. The best punishment I could think of, and damn, the only one that would make me feel, was to push you away. When my grandad died, I felt guilty. You see, he begged me not to leave for California. Called me out for only doing it for you. The money would have set us up for our dream trip. You know, the one we've talked about since we were kids.

I can show you the world.

That's what I wanted more than anything because you are the only person that has ever understood me. My grunts and utter lack of communication skills are who I am. I learned from my Grandad, and like my best friend, I too wanted a change. Wanted to meet you. Prayed I would be enough, but it was hard to believe with my hero telling me not to bother with love. That my place was here. He groomed me to take over his private business, and since my mom had stopped talking to him after a particularly bad Jameson-induced fight, he zeroed in on me. Don't get me wrong, you know I love and respect the man, but now I see the lonely life he created for himself, and I don't want that.

I want you. I want to wake up and make you coffee. Beat you to the stove so you don't burn the place down.

More than anything else, Joey, I want you to know how beautiful you are. Inside and out. You're kind and care for butt-head goats who eat your hair. Make me sandwiches when I should be making them for you. And don't even get me started on what you did for me with Billy Jean. You know more than anyone how much I love that plane, and you restored her when I was going to junk her.

Speaking of my very first plane and the reminder of Grandad. I have a surprise for you. Let the record here show that this isn't at all how I planned this, but I found a buyer. A private collector paying top dollar and Joey the money will show you the world.

I gasped reading the letter Gavin delivered this morning. A tear I didn't realize was there slides down to the paper. My heart knows every word is true, but my head won't let me forgive him yet. Does this letter make up for the harsh words he said? No. But it's a start.

I understand If you don't want to see me again. I'm so sorry I hurt our friendship, but I'm not sorry you kissed me that night in my truck. It will forever be my greatest memory. I love you, Joey, and I want you to be happy more than anything. If that's without me, I'll forward the check to whatever address you want....but if there is any part of you still willing to be patient with me and let me show you all the ways I could make you happy, then meet me out on the airstrip tomorrow morning at sunrise.

DON'T DRIVE! I got the most gut-wrenching picture of your car at the bottom of the crash site and never want to feel that helpless again. God, Joey, I know I don't deserve to know, but please tell me you're ok. You'll have a new phone at the door, and I swear you don't have to talk to me again if you'll just let me know you're not hurt.

The donuts are a bribe.... Robin will bring you tomorrow if you want to come...and because I know you love them, especially after you've been drinking. I hope you're not hurting because I was a selfish asshat. None of it was true.

You're the most amazing person I've ever met, and I was so lucky to call you mine.

Love you always. Even if I was too dumb to tell you.

Gavin.

CHAPTER EIGHTEEN

Gavin

There's a sharp chill in the air, and it bites at my nose. The sun is just beginning to peak, and the sky is an ominous spray of dark pink tones. It's still dark, and my inner asshole wants me to give up this foolish attempt.

She's never going to forgive you.

You weren't good enough to begin with. She sure as hell ain't coming back now.

Joey deserves happiness, and every fiber in my being wants to be the man to make her happy. I can't give up hope that she might love me too. If she loves me, we can move forward. I can prove to her I am a better man. A man strong enough to make positive changes in my life. To be open and talk about shit I have trouble with. Even if I have to write it down, that's what I will do because I won't push her away. I won't ignore what we have. The strong bond we've built and nurtured since we were kids. Hell, we fucking grew up being each other's rock. The partner we needed when we had a bad day or a phase where I thought liking Star Wars, and engines was gonna get my ass kicked. This was a once-in-a-lifetime love, and I know how she feels in my arms and will work every day to earn that trust back.

So here I stand. Freezing my ass off, standing in front of the Kodiak because I finalized and shipped off Billy Jean and literally have this thing loaded up to go if she says yes. If by chance I stand here all damn day without a word from her, I'm still not leaving. Tomorrow I'll take down more donuts and another letter. I'll spill my guts every fucking day until she lets me talk to her. My phone dings with a text message.

Joey: I'm ok.

She sent me a text, so I know she has the phone and read my letter.

She'll be here.

Maybe not today or next week, but fuck it, I have a wide-open schedule now and her on my mind.

What if I drive her crazy, and she hates me? What if she doesn't want a second chance with a grumpy asshole?

My insecure thoughts try to change my plans again, but then I hear the crunch of gravel, and a white car comes into view. The most beautiful face pops up above the cab when it comes to a stop.

I wave since she's still so far away I would have to shout. Does screaming I love you work in real life? Like in the movies? Would she hit me if I were to rush her and take her? Another woman might swoon, but I don't dare to manhandle my girl; she'll surely kick me in the nuts. And God, I love that about her. She is strong and going after what she wants now. Never taking shit from anyone.

Slowly she gets out and rounds the Jeep. Billy the Kid tucked under her arm. And my god, she looks fucking beautiful. She's wearing tight blue jeans and a tattered black shirt she must have gotten from Robin. But that smile I love. The one that lights up my soul isn't anywhere to be found. And that's my fault.

"Hi," she says cautiously.

"Hey."

"Got your letter."

I nod, suddenly at a loss of the right words, but knowing I need to push to find them if I stand a chance.

"I'm so sorry you had to read the other one. I never meant for you to. It was just a really low point, and all that hate was at myself, not you."

She nods, biting her lip, and Billy the Kid starts to kick in her arms, so she lets him down. The baby pygmy goat surprises me by coming straight to me. As if he missed me. The thought makes me smile. My fondness for my little buddy grew tenfold.

"He isn't the only one who cares about you, ya know. And I'm not talking about myself, but the people in your town that you always thought didn't like your grumpy personality. They do, all of them. They just respect you're a private man."

None of what she is telling me right now makes sense, and wasn't I the one that was supposed to be doing the talking?

"You know I thought I would hate this town. Furious for years thinking they were all so mean to tease you as a kid." She shakes her head, but she's not finished setting me right. "They all pulled together to get my jeep up, and they all wanted to know if there was anything they could do for Gavin's girl."

Her look is pointed. I understood it as clearly as if she read me the riot act. I never called her *my girl* to anyone. I just brought her to my bed. Never talked about us or what I wanted us to be. It was so easy, I just let us fall into a routine, but I know my mistakes now. As far as small towns go, I guess I took them all for granted. Maybe I do have more friends than I thought.

"Joey Bennett," I clear my throat, thick with emotion. "I love you. I want you to be my girl, and more importantly, I want you to feel like my girl. Billy Jean sold thanks to you, and now, if you want…." I clear my throat again. "I could show you the world."

Her bottom lip pouts, and her eyes fill with moisture. I growl and squeeze my fists tight so I don't go touching her without her permission. God, that face crushes me.

"I like your other growl better," she smiles through tears, and I can't help it anymore. I go to her. Pulling her to my chest, I am hopeful when she lets me hold her.

After a long quiet moment, she blows my mind.

"I love you, Gavin. Always have."

I gasp for air, suddenly unable to catch my breath but filled with purpose. She is mine. The woman I've loved from afar is here in my arms, and she loves me.

Her giggle at my reaction brings me out of my head and back firmly in her grasp.

"You had to know that."

"Only dared to hope."

Her smile is as bright as our future, and thank the good lord for this miracle.

"Every day, I'll prove my love, Joey. No more silence. I swear I'll tell you everything."

"I know you will, Gavin; you always have. I hear your actions loud and clear."

With that said, she pushes up on her toes and presses her soft lips to mine. I kiss her with my whole heart and soul and show her how much she means to me with my actions.

EPILOGUE

Joey

Happily ever after.

That's what they call this. Six months after Gavin told me he loved me and wanted to make a future together, I've gotten to live in this constant state of bliss.

When he found out I bought Pour Decisions, he asked if I still wanted to take our trip. I wasn't ready the day we made up; that was too much too soon. We needed to find us again. A version that wasn't friends who were secretly in love with each other, but a couple.

He took me to our waterfall for breakfast, and then we came home, where I explained I was staying forever and even invested in the town I'd fallen in love with. He was so excited he made all the calls to the city and helped get the ball rolling on the remodels I wanted.

He just stepped up beside me like it was his job to support

me. Like there wasn't anywhere else he wanted to be, not even flying around the world or rolling around naked in bed. He proves day in and day out that he wants me for me and makes me feel beautiful.

One night he bought me a dress and took me to a fancy restaurant in the city. Still don't think that's our scene, but it's part of my whole new world, and he gets that like no other person could because he's been a part of my life as I've grown and discovered the things I want.

Right now, all I want is him, but it's the opening night of the newly owned by me, Pour Decisions. To say I'm nervous and just want to sneak off and fuck my boyfriend in hopes of forgetting this silly idea altogether, well, that's an understatement.

"Joey, baby, you ready?"

"No." I smile up at the former stoic anti-social grump of the mountain. Little by little, he's realized how many of these people are his friends, and little by little, he smiles a little more.

He gives me a disapproving look that does nothing to dampen my desire to run to the back for a quickie, but I behave myself.

"I mean, yes."

"Good. Go let in all your waiting fans. They've been without a bar for four months now. I think the whole town might be ready to plow your door down."

That's not even remotely correct, with Sycamore Mountain hosting several great places to drink. I take his kind words with appreciation and reward him with a kiss I love just as much. Especially when he growls, that deep, sexy sound going straight to my core, unfurling need within me. Still, I stay strong and open the double doors, greeting each friendly face as they come up and pat me on the back or embrace me like a daughter. Each one congratulating me.

Even Robin's here, helping behind the bar because she can. The sentiment is greatly appreciated. My sassy best friend's support means more than she'll ever know.

Drinks flowing, music a steady stream of upbeat popular songs, and best of all, a smile on every face in the house. It's like a drug. Gavin's always giving me the biggest high, but being a part of this community, where no one knows me as the tomboy, or Reid's little sister, is exhilarating.

"Hey you," a familiar deep voice sounds from behind me.

"Dad!" I exclaim in surprise.

In seconds I'm wrapped in the bear hug of my childhood. The grease smell of my father sent me down memory lane. Moments later, I'm tugged by colorfully tattooed arms as Octavia hugs me tight. Then my brother pulls me under one of the boulders he calls arms, rubbing his knuckle over my head until it hurts.

"Damn it, Reid," I whine, pushing at his unmoving chest to try and get out of his grasp. He lets me go and roars with laughter.

Suddenly I turn around to find the crowded room parted, leaving an open circle of space where Gavin stands with his hands behind his back. I go to him without being called.

"Did you invite my family?"

"Maybe?"

"That's awfully sweet of you, but you really didn't have to. It's the first of many nights the bar will be open now."

"But that is a big deal, darlin'," he says, placing a chaste kiss on my nose.

A whole new world comes on over the speakers, and I gasp. Then start laughing.

"Did you request this, too?"

He nods, looking guilty but backs away instead of kissing me as I expect. Suddenly I'm frozen in place as I watch him bend the knee and pull a small black box from behind him.

The crowd hushes, and suddenly the music softens.

"Joey Bennett, you know I am a fool with words, but to be simple, I love you. I cherish you and want to honor you for the rest of our lives. Would you do me the greatest honor and be my wife?"

I burst out laughing. The crowd seems startled, and whispers begin before I can get a hold of myself, but when I do, Gavin smiles with so much joy I know my answer without a shadow of a doubt. He doesn't worry about my laughter; he encourages it.

"Yes! Yes, I want that. So much!"

He slips the gorgeous square cut diamond on my ring finger, then lifts me into the air. The crowd cheers, and my heart soars, overwhelmed with the goodness in my life.

The End

If you loved escaping to Sycamour Mountian in the other Man of the Month Club Books

Series Link: https://geni.us/SycamoreMountain

JAN 1: Snowbody but You: https://geni.us/SnowbodyButYou

JAN 15: Whiskey Throttle: https://geni.us/WhiskeyThrottle

FEB 1: Valentine Veto: https://geni.us/ValentineVeto

FEB 15: Drunk Dial: https://geni.us/DrunkDial

MAR 1: Good Times: https://geni.us/GoodTimesMOTM

MAR 15: To Hive and to Hold: https://geni.us/ToHive

APR 1: Fool's Paradise: https://geni.us/FoolsParadise

APR 15: After the Rain: https://geni.us/AfterTheRain

MAY 1: Mustard Been You: https://geni.us/MustardBeenYou

MAY 15: Because of the Brave: https://geni.us/BecauseOfTheBrave

JUN 1: Whiskey Business: https://geni.us/WhiskeyBusiness

JUN 15: Midsummer Sinners: https://geni.us/MidsummerSinners

JUL 1: The Kiss Code: https://geni.us/TheKissCode

JUL 15: Coming In Hot: https://geni.us/ComingInHot

AUG 1: His Big Book Stack: https://geni.us/HisBigBookStack

AUG 15: Love Bites: https://geni.us/LoveBitesMOTM

SEP 1: Beards and Love Letters: https://geni.us/BeardsAndLoveLetters

SEP 15: Naughty and Nice: https://geni.us/NaughtyAndNice

OCT 1: His Red Delicious: https://geni.us/HisRedDelicious

OCT 15: Bewitching You: https://geni.us/BewitchingYou

NOV 1: Fighting Ace: <u>mybook.to/fightingace</u>

NOV 15: Feast Mode: https://geni.us/FeastMode

DEC 1: Peak of Temptation: https://geni.us/
PeakOfTemptation

DEC 15: Heart's Salvation: https://geni.us/HeartsSalvation

ABOUT THE AUTHOR

HEATHER LAUREN IS a polly pocket size mom of three who only takes her book boyfriends seriously. She lives in sunny Arizona and enjoys writing steamy contemporary romance and romantic comedies with a strong cup of coffee or a sweet cocktail in hand. Listen along to your favorite book characters on the made for you playlists on Spotify and watch out for Easter eggs in all her books.

Other Books By Heather Lauren
https://www.amazon.com/Heather-Lauren/e/B08L
H8XSLZ/ref=aufs_dp_fta_dsk

Rum and Records (free)
https://storyoriginapp.com/giveaways/77ac4402-396f-
11eb-8e2e-d3776136d48e

Whiskey and Honey
https://www.amazon.com/dp/B08Q4JNFJ3

Black Velvet and Lace
https://www.amazon.com/dp/B08VJLH7WV

Vodka and Pop Rocks
https://www.amazon.com/dp/B096YZQ82Z

Absinthe and Heart
https://www.amazon.com/dp/B09C2MHB8J

Socially Awkward Series-
https://www.amazon.com/gp/product/B0925P246S?
ref_=dbs_p_mng_rwt_ser_shvlr&storeType=ebooks

Un-Swipe: an enemies to lovers romantic comedy
https://www.amazon.com/dp/B09257CP8D

Un-Like: an unrequited love/fake date romantic comedy
https://www.amazon.com/dp/B0973JF932

Un-Friend: a secret baby/road trip romantic comedy

https://www.goodreads.com/author/show/20801651.
Heather_Lauren

Interconnected Standalones

Bourbon Backroads
(Dean & Sawyer's story Graces mom and step dad)
https://www.amazon.com/dp/B09PRQZMBW

Curves For Christmas Series

The Holiday Set Up
https://www.amazon.com/dp/B09895R35B

Single Dad Santa
https://www.amazon.com/dp/B0B4MCC9XR

Holidates Series

Falling For My Holidate
(Dominic and Sophie's Story)
https://www.amazon.com/dp/B09GNSGCBJ

Bred and Butter: Baby Breeder
https://www.amazon.com/dp/B0B57WGKNN

Man of the Month Club Series Books

Beards and Books
https://www.amazon.com/dp/B08X16J98Z

Beards and Love Letters
https://www.amazon.com/dp/B09LBJFQCK

Coming Soon

Strong Man: Night Circus Series
https://www.amazon.com/dp/B0B8JY4ZXK

THANK you so much for reading Joey and Gavin's story. Joey was a spitfire from Beards and Books and imagine her surprise when she falls for a beard of her own. I loved Gavin's broken ways and how much he knew he needed Joey. He never understood how what it was like to struggle with his appearance, but it was his pleasure to reassure Joey she was beautiful.

SIGN up for my newsletter if you'd like to follow along this crazy journey! https://storyoriginapp.com/giveaways/ 77ac4402-396f-11eb-8e2e-d3776136d48e